Copyright
L. J. Tho
Pen name Li

All rights reserved, including the right to reproduce
This book, or portions therein
No parts of this book may be reproduced without
The written consent of the author
All persons in this book are fictional and any resemblance
To persons living or dead is purely coincidental
**All illustrative material used has been purchased legally,
And with the right to use in such a manner as for, but not limited to,
The purpose of book cover design. Website used is
www.canstockphoto.com**

First Published January 2015

ISBN-13: 978-1507732977
ISBN-10: 150773297X

Happy Reading

Lindsey Jayne x

Dedications

I dedicate this book to all those that have stood by me while I shed blood, sweat and tears into making it happen.

It goes without saying that the support of my family, friends and loved ones has been truly paramount in the success of my first published piece. I appreciate the time and effort they have afforded me during my goal.

I want to thank everyone that has wished me well and/or offered to test read my story before releasing it to Joe Public; old school friends, Facebook fans, other authors (whose advice and time has been insurmountable), the great people I have interacted with through author websites, Beta readers, you have all been absolutely amazing.

To all those that have injected supportive humour into backing me, bounced ideas back and forth with me, listened to me go on, and on, and on. I can't tell you enough how much you made me smile.

If I list everyone here who has really stood by me during this trial I will be here for pages and pages, and by that time you will be too bored to want to continue.

However, I will personally send my everlasting thanks and undying love to my mum, Judy, my sister, Kirsty, and my best friend, Luke. Finally, to my friend Dan, who just would not shut up about reminding me on the adverbs we discussed over multiple evenings. Your words of encouragement, your support, your fabulous marketing skills (Kirsty! Ha!), your patience and your time, none of it has gone unnoticed, and so this book is dedicated to each and every one of you. I love you all.

Preface

Wow, where does one even beginning mapping this remarkable journey? I suppose the beginning is a safe place to start.

It all began with Fifty Shades...

My partner at the time bought me E.L James's books and I was hooked. I went on to read the Crossfire novels by Sylvia Day and that was it for me – filthy, rich, alpha males! Say no more.

But, in truth, it goes even further than that. It started when I was a young girl on a trip to Scotland to visit family. My aunty, Carol, gave me her copy of The Sleepless by Graham Masterton to read while I was in bed of a night. I loved it, and from there it went on to Shaun Hutson and James Herbert.

I have no idea why, but I restricted myself to these three authors because I loved the horror elements of their books, especially if a supernatural twist was thrown in every now and again. I tended not to deviate too much, save for reading the classics like The Hobbit and Lord of the Rings by J.R.R Tolkien, too afraid I might not like what I read.

Cue Fifty Shades.

After reading my way through a couple more novels of naughty fun, Simon went one step further and bought me a Kindle Fire one Christmas. Well, it was game over after that; thousands upon thousands of books at the touch of a button. And better yet, recommendations based on my choices.

To this day, I still have hundreds of books I haven't even begun to read yet – I have a habit of seeing a collection of say eight or ten hot, alpha male stories and I am all over those like a rash! In fact, it was because of this that I discovered some of my favourite authors to date.

After reading my way through The Protector series by Teresa Gabelman, I began to consider the possibility of writing something myself. And, actually, for myself – I had no intentions of publishing or taking it any further than the experiment I intended for it to be.

But I wrote something that roughly constituted a novel. Invoking the Witch. And it was the biggest pile of rubbish I could have ever hoped to come up with. But then I used that lovely social media site we all know and love as Facebook, and I found myself someone willing to give my work a good going over. Sean Hoade – author of Deadtown Abbey (read it!). He read my first draft and after a few emails back and forth I completely re-mastered the whole manuscript, I mean the only thing that remained were the character names!

He copy edited my work, and while doing so, I discovered a fabulous website called Scribophile. I was originally looking for other people to read my work and offer reviews that I could put on the front or back cover. But what I got instead was something truly amazing. A bunch of like-minded, talented authors (or pending authors) who critiqued my work. It opened my eyes up like I couldn't even believe. Everything changed again, (albeit not quite as drastically), my flow and pacing improved and I picked up on my grammar and punctuation.

And here we have it, after months and months of meticulous tweaking, re-editing, revising, re-wording. The end hath finally arrived.

My final piece.

I have loved every single minute of creating these characters, the settings, the romance, the tension, the banter. Every bit of it! The characters (the good ones at least) are a part of a whole new fictional family and they all hold a place in my heart for one reason or another. I laughed with them, cried with them, rejoiced with them and felt their pain, and I sincerely hope you experience it, too.

I hope you all enjoy reading it as much as I have enjoyed the journey to creating it. So, ladies and gentlemen, without further ado, I give you...

Book 1 in the Faction Series

By Lindsey Jayne

Prologue

Long, black hair whipped around the High Priestess' face in the wild wind billowing through the plastic sheet-covered windows. She knelt on the concrete floor of the derelict warehouse and moved the strands aside with the gentle caress of her hand, gaze focused on the listless body on the ground. A single trickle of blood trailed from the hairline abrasion of the unconscious witch, deep crimson against her pale skin. *Dear, sweet Morgan. How easy to manipulate your damaged soul.*

"This is it, sisters. This is where supremacy begins for us." Lifting her head, the Priestess smiled at the four before her. She pulled a long, leather-handled knife from the dark robes covering her thin body; the feathers around the hilt danced in the tempestuous winds. "We cannot afford to fail now. The difficult part is over."

Her chance at justice, at retribution, presented itself here and now, and with the help of these four loyal followers she would have it.

"Years of guidance, dedication, planning. It's all been for this moment. I could not have gotten this far without you, my devoted friends. You will receive your just rewards once this is over and *she* walks among us." Her confident voice rang strong over the gusts and reverberated off the corrugated walls.

Turning to an enraptured, young brunette on the far right, the Priestess nodded. "Now, Sister Farris."

The brunette rose to her feet, brown robes swaying at her ankles as she walked with purpose across the warehouse floor to the nearest wall. She splayed her fingers over the cold surface. With quick, circular motions of her palm, the dark-haired witch repeated, "*Egredietur spriritus, ego præcipio tibi, exi foras.*"

Beneath her hand the outline of a large symbol glowed, faint at first, then bright orange. It expanded to the size of a human head before smoke spilled from the embers.

The languid haze made its way towards the raven-haired Priestess, and she grabbed hold of the thin cotton covering Morgan's belly. Knife in hand, she cut through the material with little effort and exposed the swell of the child inside.

Sister Farris sliced into her palm with a similar blade. Blood oozed and she used the slick substance to smear a sigil atop the smoky remnants of the preceding emblem. "*In nomine, Lilith,*" she whispered over and over.

The Priestess stretched forward. Grasping Morgan's limp arms, she pulled them above the prone woman's head and held them in place. The misty fog coiled tight around Morgan's thin wrists. The same went for her ankles.

The smell of scorched flesh permeated the large room. Morgan stirred, screamed pained cries. The skin on her wrists bubbled and burned through the hazy vapour.

The Priestess released her limbs. "Now!" she yelled with power and control.

"*Tace!*" Sister Farris cried out.

Sound dissolved.

Morgan writhed and thrashed on the hard ground, her screams mute.

The four advanced to kneel on the cold, concrete floor before their leader. Their wide-eyed focus settled on the Priestess.

I will not fail, I will not falter. Her coven eyed her with poised eagerness; any fear vanishing. They turned their gaze to their prisoner's wide-eyed form. The Priestess smiled down at their captive and slid the tip of her knife into Morgan's stomach to make the first incision.

∞ ∞ ∞

With a speed born of purpose, the five women shed their dark gowns and ascended the hill, against howling winds and lashing rain.

Dressed in white threads—the saturated material tight against their soaked, slippery bodies—they stayed closed to one another. Concentration fixed on their route; they ignored the mud and blood caking their bare feet while they trudged across the uneven terrain, over large tree roots, steep inclines, and jagged, stony outcrops.

The Priestess, at the front, carried a screaming bundle wrapped in the same white cloth they wore. With every clap of thunder ringing through the dense woodland, the bundle cried louder.

Darkness swamped the forest, and the full moon cast brief glimpses of light through the thick foliage.

A clearing came into view, circled by rocks of various sizes. All but the Priestess arranged themselves in formation using the boulders to stand on. The Priestess' wet, ebony hair and sodden robes stopped thrashing, rain ceased to bead off her bronzed skin the moment she stepped foot over the formation's perimeter.

Before a shallow ditch, dead centre, she crouched down, laying the stricken child inside while the rest of her acolytes stripped naked. She pulled a knife from her rags, and moonlight bounced off the sharpened blade before she drew it across her outstretched palm.

Dark crimson fluid seeped out. It dripped onto the infant, a slow, thick trail down his body before it soaked through cloth and seeped into the dank mud. Balling her hand into a fist, she moved it around the ditch. Blood pumped to create a glimmering circle. Once complete, she stripped down, bound her wound and joined the rest of her coven.

Re-entering the storm, the Priestess mounted one of the large stones. The torrential downpour beat against her bare skin, whipping wind caused goose bumps to ripple across her body.

"It is time to call for her. To offer her the first of many," she shouted above the windstorm.

The five closed their eyes and stretched their arms towards the full moon. Rain continued to hammer off the ground and bounce off their bodies. The relentless pounding of the storm tousled with their hair and it beat around their faces like sharp, stinging whips.

The group remained quiet, waiting. The child wailed over the storm. A streak of lightning brightened the skies above them, followed by a clap of thunder. The baby cried louder.

The Priestess yelled, "He cries for thee, Lilith. He is pure, untouched by the three. Come for his innocent soul. Pacify the wrongs done to thee."

Dirt and leaves blew from the ground as the wind grew stronger. An owl hooted over the din and the five began their chant,

> *"Omnes te invocamus Lilith.*
> *Omnes te invocamus Lilith*
> *Afferte, si quid tenebrarum."*

Fierce gusts created havoc outside the centre of the circle, roaring like wild beasts while flying debris collided with trees and rock. The baby's cries became more urgent and the chants grew louder,

*"Omnes te invocamus Lilith
Egressus est ad nos."*

With a cry, Sister Farris dropped to the ground, eyes still closed. On hands and knees, she crawled through wet grass and oily mud to the centre, to the baby. Removing him from the hole, she held him above her head. For long minutes, the child remained raised before the moon, the chants dying to a whisper.

Returned to the ground, the child quieted. He stared at the witch before him. With a snap, Sister Farris's head flew forwards, eyes enlarged, and baring milky-white orbs.

Eyes fixed on the infant, she took hold of his neck.

"Lilith, offero me ipsum tibi. Accipe munusculum. Largire mihi tenebrarum," she whispered to him.

Raising her head to stare at the moon, her eyes pearlescent spheres, her grip tightened.

Chapter 1

Detective Chief Inspector Amelia Ellis leaned back against her chair and waved a hand in front of her face. Muggy air swirled around the DCI's humid, Blackburn office.

Staring at decision logs and other case documentation with distaste, Amelia remembered why she preferred to be outside of her office. But no-one liked to piss off the boss, Detective Chief Superintendent Riley Thomas, by cutting corners—especially when he stood over six feet tall with the build of a Latvian shot-putter.

An incoming call on her internal phone line indicated the luxury of avoiding him before she finished, remained a pipedream.

"Ellis," she answered with blunt professionalism.

"Ellis, Thomas here." His deep voice held a hard edge.

"What can I do for you, sir?"

"I have a job for you. It's come down from the Faction."

Great. 'On loan' to a group of paranormal-hunting vampires with a God complex.

"Go on," she sighed.

"There's been a murder. It looks ... supernatural."

No shit, Sherlock. Since the paranormal exposed themselves a decade ago, her workload increased tenfold. Vampires loose with uncontrollable bloodlust, werewolves with schizophrenic tendencies and paranoid delusions, witches who managed to cock up simple protection spells and trap several of their coven in giant plastic cages. A few of the unusual things Amelia bore witness to.

"Who do I need to contact?"

"The General is running the show, but for now, you need to take your guys and meet Nate at the crime scene." He reeled off the address to her.

The no-nonsense General—Lucas Drake— led Lancashire's Faction group. Vampires were not the only supernatural creatures under his employ— humans, witches, werewolves, everyone got equal opportunity. Nate acted as head coordinator and lead investigator during daylight hours. Being a big believer in equality made Lucas a legendary leader amongst his aides.

Amelia dialled Nate's number the moment Thomas hung up, and a deep, rough voice answered within seconds.

"Yeah?"

Amelia rolled her eyes. "Nate? It's Ellis—"

"Oh, Inspector Ellis, nice of you to call. Can I expect you any time soon? I have a stab victim awaiting your expertise. Take your time; she's not going anywhere."

Smug, sarcastic bastard...

"I've just been informed. I'm gonna gather my guys, then I'll be over."

"Can't wait, gorgeous. I've missed your face."

... Urgh, but your charms are about as effective as a chocolate teapot on me, sweetheart. She hung up and shook her head, pursing her lips.

Amelia made one more call before she went in search of her team. Running a hand through her long hair, she waited for the other person to pick up.

"Simms."

Fairly new to the force, but a team player, Constable Darcy Simms made a competent officer. Young, willing to learn and great with a computer. Amelia liked her.

"Just the person. I need to go out to a scene, but I have some paperwork to finish for Thomas by the end of shift. It's the Farrow case we worked. Do you think you'd be able to complete it for me? It's nothing too extensive, just dotting the i's and crossing the t's."

"Yeah, that's not a problem, ma'am. Just pop it in on your way out. I'll have it done in no time."

"You're a star. I'll be down shortly."

Outside of the office, Amelia found her team in one of the briefing rooms.

Detective Inspector Sam Chapman, Amelia's loyal DI for the past three years, waited for her arrival. A big guy at six foot, full of muscle and tattoos with a mouthy sense of humour.

Sergeant Chloe Roberts stood talking to him. She joined eighteen months ago and the other officers gave her a hard time. She came from money and spoke with a rather 'posh' accent. But the chatty, shrewd red-head didn't let it get her down, instead using her quick wit to give as good as she got.

Both good officers, Amelia thanked her lucky stars for her team.

"We've been 'let out' to the Faction again. Nate's waiting for us on site with a stab victim." Amelia figured she might as well be blunt about it—they weren't going to like it, either, but they didn't have a choice. "No other details as of yet."

"We'd best not keep the grump waiting, then?" Chloe quipped.

∞ ∞ ∞

Amelia took Chloe in her blue Vauxhall Astra while Sam hopped onto his blue and white Suzuki GSX R1000 motorbike and roared off in front of them.

"Jackass." Chloe shook her head and chuckled.

"Aw, let him have his fun. He saved up for that beauty like his life depended on it," Amelia smiled.

"Yes, and I never heard the end of it. 'I can't go out with my mates tonight,' 'I can't take this really hot girl out,' 'I can't take this other really hot girl out.' He bored me to tears." Chloe mimicked Sam in a voice a few octaves higher than necessary.

Amelia laughed at her. "He still can't take really hot girls out. Where they gonna sit?"

"Oh, don't even get me started on his 'ride me' jokes. I wanted to punch him."

*

It didn't take long for Amelia and Chloe to pull up behind Nate's battered old van parked on a dilapidated industrial site full of decayed, empty warehouses.

"How is he not embarrassed to be driving around in that knackered, old death trap?" Chloe mused aloud.

"You've seen him, right? Scruffy hair, bum fluff all over his face, clothes hanging off his arse. It would be difficult to imagine him driving anything else."

"Good point. I suppose we'd best go find him."

Exiting the car, they walked around Nate's van to find him and Sam all but drooling over the bike. Amelia rolled her eyes—*men.*

"Put 'em back in your pants, boys. Where's the vic?"

"DCI Ellis, looking as ravishing as ever." Nate stood up tall and turned on the charm within seconds.

Sam smirked and dismounted his bike.

Amelia knew Nate's game—and his reputation—a self-confessed ladies' man. She could see why women fell for him. Nate's tall build, naturally tanned skin and dark hair and eyes made him very attractive. He did have a scruffy look to him, with his trendy surfer-style haircut that swept over his deep eyes and his "couldn't care less" attitude over what oversized, tatty attire he decided to wear. But he pulled it off well.

"Cut the crap, Nate, we're here to work. Where's the body?"

He smiled a dimpled grin and extended an invitation for her to go on ahead, eyeing the sway of her hips while she sauntered up to him.

Running a hand over the light stubble on his chin, he gave Amelia an appreciative grin and she caught sight of his angled hand, poised to pat her backside before she sidled past him.

"Do it, and I'll rip your arm off and smack you with it."

"Feisty," Nate growled at her with a smirk.

The four of them walked into a crumbling warehouse.

"Young, female vic, gutted throat to groin, and she *was* pregnant. No sign of the baby." Nate's matter-of-fact tone left no room for emotions.

The three officers stopped in their tracks, Chloe's brow furrowing. Nate bumped into Amelia's back with an "oomph" before taking the opportunity to cop a feel of her arse. She didn't care at that moment, focused only on the gruesome news he just delivered.

"I beg your pardon? She was slit open, and the child was removed?" She spun around to face him.

"Yup." Nate sounded casual and unaffected. "I've taken pictures and gathered all the evidence."

"So, why do we need to be here?" Amelia cocked her head in query.

If he made any smarmy comment about how he wanted to see her face or whatever, she'd blind him with her own fingers.

"The scene's a bit ... strange. There's definitely witchcraft involved, and I know you're pretty hot with that topic. I thought you could take a look, see what you think."

Amelia nodded. "Roberts, you gonna be OK with this?"

Chloe paled, but nodded. Her experience so far didn't stretch to gruesome murder scenes, but this would be something she'd need to deal with—best to suck it up now, and get it over with.

Amelia turned to back Nate, raised her eyebrows, and swept her hand in front of her.

Following Nate toward the back of the warehouse, Amelia came over uneasy.

The air around her grew thick and heavy with the aftermath of murder, yet everything remained eerily still, aside from the occasional creak and groan. Plastic coverings over the windows flapped in sporadic bursts amid quick gusts of air trying to permeate the gloom. Their footsteps echoed off the corrugated walls.

A darkened room extended off the main warehouse, a cloying, ominous ambience hung in the area within.

Outside the entrance, Nate stopped. Amelia saw light flicker inside—candles, perhaps? The stench of blood and death lingered. After a few deep breaths, she covered her nose and walked through the doorless entryway, the deathly silence palpable.

Larger than first thought, the room shone with the glow of several spluttering candles, in various states of use—puddles of dried wax surrounded those distinguished. Numerous colourful cushions lay in disarray towards the centre encircled by a large white-powdered symbol. The salt circle, used by witches to keep evil spirits and demons at bay, lay broken.

A coven likely gathered in this warehouse to chant and pray.

Snapping on a pair of latex gloves, Amelia ambled toward the scene against the far wall. Adjacent to the circle, it contained the more disturbing evidence; the metal wall itself smeared in a dark, drying liquid—blood. Lots of it; its coppery tang hung in the air.

Burnt in the wall and caked in flaky blood, a cryptic symbol depicted a crescent moon above an upside-down cross. Amelia noted the distinct smell of rotted meat coming from the smoky remains. It penetrated the fetid odour of the slaughter that took place—the horror of which she now stared at.

Beneath the smouldering symbol lay the body of a woman, horror in her eyes made more gruesome from the shadows dancing about her face and the gnawed, bloodied teeth marks from the vermin who made a feast of her flesh. Her hands lay above her head, fused together, skin raw. Her legs spread apart at an unnatural angle and bruises formed around the joints, highlighted by her ashen skin.

Taking two steps closer, Amelia glared at the gaping hole in the woman's stomach. Thick blood pooled from it into a congealed mass beneath the poor soul. The jagged edges of the flesh looked scorched, cauterised. Shifting her gaze to the woman's wrists and ankles, Amelia noticed angry, red scald marks around each one.

The wrists bore the brunt of the damage. Whatever caused the burns melted the skin on each wrist together to form one big mass of bloodied, blistered flesh.

"Jesus," Sam exclaimed.

Amelia flinched. Morbidly mesmerised by the scene, she didn't hear Sam approach behind her. She turned to Nate and Chloe, having wandered in.

"T.O.D., Nate?"

"Liver temp puts her time of death roughly seven hours ago. Around midnight."

"Theories?"

Nate shook his head. "It's dark magic, that's for sure. But by who and for what purpose… well, that's where you come in."

"That symbol," Amelia nodded her head in the direction of the wall, "I don't recognise it, do you?"

"Afraid not, Doll. Maybe we'll have some luck searching the archives." He wandered closer to the remains. "What do you make of the condition of her wrists?" He proceeded.

"Demonic, for sure, but we'll know more when we get the samples back for testing." Amelia pointed at the smouldering symbol. "That's got something to do with the marks on our victim's wrists and ankles, I can assure you." Turning to Sam, she challenged, "Initial thoughts?"

He circled the body and surmised, "Black magic. The vic wasn't here alone to start with. She was meditating with others. They left, the murderer pounced. She knew her attacker because the scene isn't disturbed. There's no sign of any struggle until the victim was restrained."

"Good. What about the nature of the wounds, Roberts?" Amelia cocked her head in the ashen Sergeant's direction.

Chloe swallowed hard before she dropped to crouch beside the body. "The incisions are fairly precise; the murderer remained calm. They knew what they were doing. The weapon has some kinks in it, though, because the tool marks aren't completely straight."

Kneeling to join her colleague, Amelia searched the corpse with slow, measured focus. She grabbed a small torch from her jacket pocket and shone it across the remains several times. "The weapon used was a sacrificial blade."

"How do you know?" Nate switched his gaze from the DCI to the victim's stomach.

"They're scorched; the blade was enchanted before it was used. But, more importantly… you missed one vital clue."

"I did? No way." Having the good grace to look astounded, Nate moved closer.

Fishing some tweezers from the small kit she carried, Amelia bent further over the woman's corpse, recoiling at the noxious stench before she delved into the grisly wound. She offered Nate the two centimetre piece of bone she held. He stretched out a gloved hand for Amelia to drop the article in.

"What is it?" Sam stepped closer.

"It's a fragment of a knife. My guess, is it's made from human bone, and the only knives made from human bone in a witch's circle are sacrificial ones."

"Shit. I assumed it was just a fragment of one of the vic's bones." Nate turned the evidence over between his fingers.

"You know what they say about assuming, Nate. It's a good thing you called me then." Amelia cocked a smile at him. "How you thought it belonged to her is beyond me, it was lodged *in between* the bones of her second and third rib. Also, look at the distinct discoloration and the sharp tip. You can see where it's been carved into a point."

"And you wonder why we need you here." Nate grinned back at her. "Sebastian woulda found it, though." He winked.

"Um, guys. I hate to rain on both your parades, but you've missed something else." Sam hovered over the woman's face.

Amelia and Nate turned, the DCI curious. "What is it, Chapman?" His boss crouched next to him.

"See how her trachea is protruding slightly? Unless she's a transvestite, there's something wedged in there."

Amelia bent over the victim, pried her lips open and retrieved the object stuck in her throat. Pulling it out, she held it up to the light. "A bird claw?"

"A what ... ?" Nate glanced at Amelia. "Is it an owl's claw?"

"If I were to guess right now, then yeah, I'd say so."

"Puts things into perspective. We should get back to the Compound, we got research to do."

"You're going to have to be a bit more specific, mate," Sam interjected.

At the warehouse exit, Nate stopped while he ran a hand over his stubble. "Millie's right. This does involve the sacrifice of babies, and it won't be stopping at one. Someone's trying to resurrect a demon."

Chapter 2

"You should go. Daniel will be home soon." I hung my head and stared at my interlaced fingers resting on the light oak kitchen table. I caught sight of a fading bruise and pulled down the sleeve of my jumper to further hide it.

"And? Ellie... ," Alice sighed, shrugging her shoulders. "Okay, but call me when you get back, all right?"

Nodding, I kept my gaze averted. I couldn't look her in the eyes. I imagined her eyes burning into me with accusation and pity.

Daniel and I would be leaving in the morning for a weekend away together. A last short holiday while he could afford the time off work, and before I gave birth to our daughter. Our first child together and my last shred of hope.

I didn't want things to return to the way they were after she arrived.

"Listen, sweetheart. I know you said you weren't sure about a christening or anything, but my mom called me today and offered you the function room free of charge. If you want it."

Set against a backdrop of gorgeous Lancashire countryside, their beautiful Georgian Establishment offered a perfect location for my daughter's christening. Alice's parents and I had formed a close relationship over the years and I appreciated their offer, but I couldn't accept.

"I don't think Daniel is too keen on the idea," I murmured.

"And what about you, what do you want?"

My face heated, anxious palpitations gripped me at her accusatory tone. "It's not just Daniel; I'm not big on the whole religion thing either. I just don't see the point in going through with a ceremony where none of the beliefs mean anything to me."

In truth, while I didn't practice the religion, the rest of the process excited me; the pretty dresses, the gorgeous gifts, the excuse for a party. But Daniel wouldn't have liked all the fuss. He just wanted a quiet life with us, his family. We didn't need an excuse to throw away unnecessary expense on a party.

"Well, the offer's there if you want it, love."

Alice rose from her chair at the kitchen table, grabbed her bag off one of the black marble units, and made for the front door, with me in tow.

"Thanks for the brochures. Daniel and I will have a look through them later."

"You're welcome. Call me when you get a minute, okay? I wanna hear all about it."

She pulled me in for a hug. My stiff body loosened in her arms before she held me back and beamed an infectious smile at me.

Climbing into her red Mini Cooper, she waved at me and drove away. I shut the door and walked back to the kitchen. The brochures she brought around were splayed out on the table—activity brochures for the getaway to Cornwall that Daniel and I would be taking. I scooped them up and shoved them to the bottom of the bin. Being very well organised, Daniel already planned our activities.

With the catalogues binned, I made sure to wash, dry and put away our mugs, clear the table and hoover the charcoal-tiled floor. A house-proud Daniel hated for things to look untidy or unclean.

Once done, and certain I cleaned the rest of our two-bed semi-detached with the same thoroughness, I went upstairs to continue packing. We were to spend two blissful days soaking up the Cornish sun and relaxing on the beautiful Devonshire beaches.

Daniel's job in real estate demanded a lot of his time. With that and the baby, we both needed this break. Once our little girl arrived, Daniel would only have a couple of weeks to help me and to bond with his daughter before returning to work.

I didn't need to work; when I met a twenty-four year-old Daniel, he'd told me he would provide for me. I quit my job at Alice's parent's pub, and, at eighteen, settled into creating a home for him.

Now at twenty-one, I couldn't complain. I cradled my massive, seven-month bump and smiled. I couldn't wait to meet the daughter nestled in there. I often wondered which of us she would look like. Would she have my light brown hair and chocolate eyes? Or would they be darker, like Daniel's? Would her lips be thick and voluptuous like mine? Would she have gorgeous high cheekbones like her father? Excitement swam through me and I smiled.

Daniel's key in the front door knocked me from my daydream. The thud of his briefcase drummed off the carpeted floor before his footsteps padded down the hallway.

"Ellie, where are you?"

"I'm up here," I shouted to him.

Bounding up the steps, he crossed the landing to our room. His tall, muscular frame stood in the doorway. Dark, slicked-back 'business-hair' damp from the drizzle outside. I could barely make out his once captivating, deep green eyes while they observed me from under furrowed brows.

"What are you doing?" A note of distaste stained his question.

"I'm packing, silly." I smiled while I folded another skirt and placed it in the suitcase that lay across our white-wood bed.

"What did you call me?" He lowered his tone, full of malice.

Shit. I panicked. My body shivered ice cold.

"I'm sorry, darling. I was only joking." With hurried words, I hoped I righted my wrong. *What else do I say, it just slipped out?* Anxiety gripped me in a tight vice.

"Think before you speak, Elora. You're not *that* stupid."

"I'm sorry," I muttered again.

"Why are you packing alone? I thought we were going to do it together." His condescending tone soaked into my skin and caused me to shudder.

"Would you like me to stop? We can do it after we've eaten." *When will I learn?*

"What have you made for dinner?"

Relieved by the change in subject, I replied in haste, "I've made a lasagne. Is that okay?"

"I suppose." He couldn't have looked more disinterested, his stoic expression firmly fixed.

I contained the sigh before it escaped my lips. After his difficult day, I tried not to take his blasé demeanour to heart—stress caused it, and I only made it worse.

I made for the door. Daniel grabbed my upper arm in a strong grip; so strong I almost yelped in pain as his fingers pinched the fleshy part of my bicep.

He pulled me into his hard chest with such brute force a painful twinge lanced through my belly. I squinted my eyes against the tender throb.

Up until now, he'd been careful not to physically hurt me in case anything happened to the baby, and I prayed this wasn't the start of it again. His virile, bullish behaviour continued, but his laying a finger on me had calmed.

He stared at me for interminable moments. His look, however difficult to read, appeared neither loving nor kind, so when he forced his lips over mine, confusion reigned. I tried not to grimace at the impassioned urgency while he forced me backwards and all but pushed me out the door.

I stumbled onto the landing, and he slammed the door behind me. I stood stock still and blinked hard, running plausible excuses for his behaviour through my brain—pressure from work, my pregnancy hormones.

A kick from our daughter reminded me that she would soon be here, and so I made my way downstairs to prepare his dinner.

∞ ∞ ∞

We made our way upstairs after a dinner spent enduring an uncomfortable silence. I contained my gasp at the entire contents of my suitcase emptied on the grey carpeted floor.

"Elora, some of the things you packed were highly inappropriate. You can put them away now."

"What do you mean?" The question left my lips before I realised I should've kept my damn mouth shut.

"Are you questioning my judgment? I know what's good for you. Haven't I looked after you well enough by now?"

I nodded, weak. "You're absolutely right. Come on, we'll get this done together."

Appeased by my statement, he moved to my wardrobe to remove clothes he deemed suitable. After all, he planned the whole trip, even down to our activities; he knew better what I needed.

It didn't take him long to stuff my suitcase with suitable attire. I didn't check what he packed. He wouldn't have liked me undermining his judgment.

Daniel made his way downstairs while I opted to take a shower. I wanted to be fresh for the next day's travel, but I didn't want to spend too much time on it in the morning; Daniel would want to leave sharpish.

Shedding my T-shirt and jeans, his voice boomed out, "Elora, get down here right now!"

Oh God. I did not like the livid tone laced through his words.

Wasting no time, I ambled down the stairs—wrapped in a white towel—with all the speed I could muster, despite my condition. Daniel stood over the kitchen table, the collection of Alice's brochures splayed across it. *Damn,* I knew I should've taken them straight outside. I shivered while I waited for the ensuing argument.

I hesitated in the kitchen doorway—Daniel's face blood red with rage—and I prayed my shaking body went undetected. I didn't want to succeed in making my mistake a whole lot worse.

"I can explain." The uncomfortable silence encouraged me to utter something, while his wide eyes bore into me.

"Go on." He spoke slow, purposeful, through gritted teeth.

"Alice thought she was helping, that's all. She didn't know you'd already thought it all through, and I hadn't the heart to tell her, after the effort she went to." My words were panicked, hurried.

He glared at me. My body quaked and my skin prickled. I clutched the towel, holding the hem tight against my breasts.

"What was *she* doing here?" He stood tall and his chest heaved with every breath he took, jaw pulsating through clenched teeth.

"Sh-she came around to drop those off, that's all." I pointed, trembling with fear, at the array of catalogues on the table.

"Do you think I'm stupid? I don't know why you still give her the time of day. She doesn't like me, and she doesn't want to see you happy." Venom spiked his patronising tone. "She fills your head with poison, wants to turn you against me. She is not to come into this house anymore, do you understand?"

He grabbed a handful of the brochures and threw them in my direction, screaming profanities at me. I raised my arms to protect my face, but the catalogues never made it all the way over to me.

My body shook when he marched over to me, his nostrils flared, his eyes wide with malicious intent.

He got close to my face and his large hands grasped my upper arms in a tight hold. He hissed at me, "Why am I not enough for you?"

I stared at him while throbbing pain ebbed through my shoulders. My vocal chords refused to form anything approaching a sentence. I stuttered, but nothing coherent came out.

Seeing this side of him again put the fear of God into me. I needed to calm him down before he did something regrettable.

His face reddened further, body tensed, his eyes glazed over.

Releasing his hold on me, he balled up a hand, and his jaw clenched and unclenched. Without warning his fist flew past my face and punched a hole in the wall beside me. I jumped.

Too scared to scream, to cry, I held my breath as my eyes welled up. Staring at his emotionless expression, I didn't dare let out a breath. I closed my eyes and the first tears fell.

Daniel barged past me, stomping upstairs, leaving me to piece together what I might've done to fuel the fires he'd kept under control for the past seven months.

Trembling against the wall for endless minutes, my brain clicked and whirred a million times per second.

Frightened, numb and confused, I put his outburst down to his job and my pregnancy. Structural issues with a property nearby shouldered him with a lot of responsibility, the pressure weighed on him daily. Frustration must be what set him off. My pregnancy hormones, aches and pains only added to the tension.

I cradled my swollen belly. When our daughter arrived, he would get better—with no other family, Daniel's eager anticipation convinced me of that. I understood his anxieties so, resolved myself to being nicer to him.

Putting the kettle on, I spooned a couple of heaped teaspoons of chocolate powder into large mugs—he liked to have a warm drink to go to bed with.

Pouring the water in, I stirred the beverages and picked up the two steaming cups before I made my way to our bedroom.

Daniel lay in bed, and I placed his mug beside him, on the bedside drawer before I walked around to my side and did the same.

After I changed into my nightshirt, I climbed under the blue-grey covers and propped myself against the headboard.

Daniel lay down his book and turned to me. "You're too good for me, Elora. I don't know why you put up with me."

I returned a weak smile.

"You must know the pressure I'm under at work, but maybe your pregnancy is scrambling your brain. I know you won't do it again."

Guilt shadowed me at my carelessness.

"I'm sorry, Daniel. I don't think sometimes--"

"I know you don't. It's okay, though. We've talked about it and you know better now." He picked up his book to signify the end of the matter.

I looked at him like a child reprimanded. He ignored my gaze, his expression impassive. *The holiday will mellow him out, he just needs to relax,* I thought to myself, while I lay down.

"Don't forget your drink. You know I don't like to see things wasted." He didn't even take his eyes off his book.

Of course, how mindless of me. I sat, grabbed my drink, and took long gulps.

"Not too fast. You'll burn the back of your throat."

My cheeks flared at his parent-to-child scolding. I couldn't bring myself to look at him while I took smaller sips—he wouldn't have bothered to look at me when he spoke.

After a few agonising minutes, I finished my drink and lay back down. Daniel, satisfied, remained silent. After several more minutes, he closed his book, turned his bedside light off, and lay down next to me. I didn't have a lamp on my side, Daniel preferred it that way; I couldn't keep him awake with it.

He moved closer to my back and put his arm over me, caressing my bump.

"I love you, darling. I can't wait to meet our daughter. She's going to change our lives."

While I drifted off to sleep, I wondered why his words left a bitter taste in my mouth.

Chapter 3

The shrill sound of Daniel's alarm woke us both. He stirred beside me before he reached over to switch it off. I started to get up, but he turned back and put his arm around me, nuzzling his face into my neck. My shoulder pulsed.

"Mmm, five more minutes."

I smiled. "Okay, but we both know you don't like to be late."

Daniel tensed, and his arm cut deep into my belly. I yelped at the debilitating cramp as it shot through my stomach.

"Don't tell me what I like," he sniped at me, face so close to my ear I could feel the heat and almost taste the venom laced through his words.

His arm remained clamped over my stomach. My little girl didn't like it because I could feel her. She writhed around inside me, kicked and squirmed.

"Daniel, I'm sorry. Please let me go… the baby."

"Oh, the baby will be fine, you daft cow. You're too paranoid, that's your problem. Don't take me for a dick, Elora."

"I-I'm sorry... I never... ."

Launching himself out of bed, he stomped towards the en-suite. "You're pathetic."

Two words, but the hurt and shame ran deep. I *am* pathetic. I wanted to cry, but I didn't want to give him the satisfaction, nor the ammunition to throw more accusations my way. Instead, I got up and shuffled toward the guest bathroom when I heard Daniel switch our shower on.

*

An hour later we were both ready to go, having uttered no more than a few words to one another. I did my best to avoid him and his increasingly fickle temperament all morning. I began to dread this holiday.

I made us a few snacks, but Daniel wanted to stop at a service station along the way to pick up some other little nibbles. I didn't have a problem with that, not that I'd have voiced it anyway, but I wanted to grab a few magazines to read. The five-hour journey would be quite uncomfortable for me; I needed something to occupy my mind.

We packed Daniel's black Audi A7 with our suitcases and other odds and ends he deemed necessary, climbed in, and set off. Adjusting my seat, I grabbed my travel pillow to support my neck. I cast Daniel an inconspicuous glance to see his rigid expression, jaw tense, concentration fixed on the road in front of him.

An hour or so into the drive, we pulled into a service station to stretch our legs. Once inside, Daniel headed for the café, while I went to relieve my bladder before I made my way into the shop to get a few sweets and reading material for the journey.

I waited in the short line to pay and caught Daniel stalking towards me, steaming drink in hand.

"What you getting?" he asked me in a bland tone.

I smiled and held up my purchases—two bags of sweets and four magazines.

His face dropped, and my stomach along with it.

"What the hell do you want those for? Sweets aren't good for you, and is my company not enough? Do I bore you?"

He may have hissed his words at me—audible only to those in close proximity—but my face ignited all the same. I wanted the ground to swallow me whole—those close to me tried hard to look anywhere else, and I felt nauseous. Opening my mouth to say something, the words caught in my dry throat.

"Put all of those back. Now. You don't need them." Grabbing my arm he yanked me out of the queue before he turned to address the strangers in it, "Sorry for the inconvenience she's caused."

No one said a word; they just stared, dumbstruck, at the spectacle before them. Humiliated, I burst into tears. Daniel grabbed the goods from my hands and threw them on the nearest shelf before he strong-armed me back to the car, binning his cup on the way.

I climbed in seconds before Daniel, who slammed his door with force.

"What the hell did you think you were doing in there? Now those people think I'm a spiteful bastard. Why did you make me do that?"

Sniffling, I stammered, "I-I... they're strangers... w-we don't--"

"Oh, stop snivelling, you whiny brat. I can't believe you did that to me. You're a selfish bitch at the best of times. Clean yourself up, you look a mess."

Humiliation surged through me while I reached for the glove compartment for tissues.

"Shit. No, Elora--"

The compartment door opened and a strange-looking knife bounced off my foot, handle first, and fell to the floor.

A gasp caught in my throat. My stomach turned and my face went cold. Why did Daniel have a knife in his car? About eight inches long, it didn't look like an ordinary knife; tied to the cork-like shaft, varying coloured feathers splayed out, metal rungs adorned the centre. Etchings were carved into the sharp-looking ivory blade—like runes.

I jumped when Daniel snatched hold of it, shoved it down the side of his seat, and slammed the glove box closed.

"What the hell do you think you're doing, rifling through my things?" Chest heaving with each erratic breath, his face reddened.

"I-I was looking for a tissue." My tears stopped from the shock settling in, but my body still trembled. "What--"

"None of your fucking business."

"But--"

"Well, there's no point in going away now, look at you. What a complete waste, you've cost me again." He slammed the palms of his hands on the steering wheel, let out a frustrated growl and turned on the ignition. "Always the fucking martyr. I'm not taking you anywhere with you acting like the victim; we're going home."

Hot tears resumed their trail down my cheeks and I wiped them away with shaky hands.

Wrenching the car into gear, we screeched away from the service station as the tires left a smoky trail behind us.

The journey home stretched out. Nervous and scared, I swallowed down bile several times, my mouth dry, but

I didn't dare move even to grab a drink of water. I barely took a decent breath in case the sound annoyed him somehow.

I attempted to go over the past twenty-four hours. Daniel's returning violence scared me—I dealt with it in the past, but for it to come back full circle, after so many months of hoping... and now the knife!? Any excuses I could make for his behaviour, or had made, dissipated the more I thought about it. And the more I thought about it, the sicker I felt.

Daniel made some calls to cancel our reservations. For every single one he blamed me. The car-Bluetooth set meant I heard every word of the two-way conversations; every giggled apology from the beguiled women, every comment about how much deposit he'd lose from the empathetic men, every bitter remark about how he'd be sure I understood just how much I'd cost him.

I tried to fathom how I ever thought this behaviour could be deemed normal. The only time I could recall being truly ecstatic was finding out about my pregnancy, not that Daniel even bothered turning up to my doctor's to support me for the first visit, or any of the scans since.

I would be left alone a lot; in the house while he worked, all by myself when he went out for drinks, alone when he celebrated going into business for himself, God forbid *I* wanted to do something. Shopping happened when he became available, or I did it online under his watchful eye. If I wanted to visit my dad, he would have to tag along. Spending time with Alice—the only friend left who refused to let his possessive behaviour drive her away—proved near impossible. Anger and resentment began to stir. Because of him.

He came into *my* life, made me feel isolated, ashamed, and worthless. Pig-headed, selfish, controlling arsehole, always finding a way to blame me. *He* chose to stay with *me,* even though he berated and belittled me every single day. Who else would be his obedient little lapdog, listen to his obnoxious whining while he threw his weight around? Until now, only me. Too weak for my own good. Well, no more.

My bravado wavered when we turned onto our street. My little moment of self-realisation did wonders for my state of mind, but did I really have it in me to call him out? He had a knife in his car, for crying out loud. I turned to look at him; his hands gripped the steering wheel, knuckles white from the pressure, chest heaving with each heavy breath he took. His jaw pulsated, nostrils flared.

Daniel put the car into park on our drive and nigh-on catapulted himself from the vehicle. Absolute fear rooted me to the spot while Daniel threw the front door open and chucked our suitcases into the hallway with a strength born of rage. Still I didn't move. He wrenched the passenger-side door damn near off its hinges.

"Get out! Now!"

With leaden fingers I unbuckled my seat belt and scrambled from the car into the house like a frightened little puppy, tail between its legs.

Straight-backed on the brown, upholstered sofa in our cream-papered lounge, I dug my hands into my lap, eyes trained on a spot somewhere on the light carpet.

The front door slammed shut, and Daniel stalked through the hallway to stand under the arch connecting it to the lounge. I looked up.

His shoulders moved up and down at an alarming rate. A result of him heaving all the luggage into the house, or seething with pure hatred and fury? I didn't feel it necessary to ask.

With his lips set firm, I stared at him wide-eyed. "Daniel... why do you have a knife in your car?"

"Why not? What the hell would you know, anyway?" He remained still, his jaw pulsed. "It's a collector's item."

"You collect knives?"

"Yes."

"But why do you keep one in your car?"

He shrugged and raised a brow.

"Stop acting so relaxed, Daniel. You have a knife in your car that you obviously didn't want me to see. If it had been something as immaterial as you're making it out to be, then you wouldn't have cancelled our holiday."

My heart skipped a beat—I didn't clam up, I stood my ground... until he flew over to me. Leaning my back against the arm of the sofa, I cowered when Daniel shoved his face in mine.

"You don't know anything about me, you ignorant bitch." His face a contorted mask of ferocity—his bulging eyes gave him a demented look.

"W-w-what do you mean?" My voice quaked beyond control.

Pulling back, he laughed in my face, a blood-churning sound. Fresh waves of nausea swirled in my stomach. This change in Daniel petrified me.

Without another word he stormed to his office and slammed the door open against the wall, the vibrations caused the frames dotted along the walls to rattle. I considered—before he charged back in—bolting for the front door, but he'd get to me before I managed to shuffle far enough toward it, and I feared his reaction.

"Get up," he barked through clenched teeth, his lips curled up.

Lifting myself off the sofa, I yelped when he seized my wrist—bone creaking under the pressure while his fingernails dug into my skin.

"Daniel, wha--"

He propelled me toward the bottom of the stairs. "Take your shit upstairs and get it unpacked. I'll be damned if I'm sorting through it, again."

Wide-eyed and focused on his red face, I didn't move. He couldn't expect me to haul my case upstairs in my condition. I opened my mouth to say something, but only a whimper escaped.

"What the fuck are you waiting for?" He gestured toward the case and flung a pointed finger in the direction of the stairs. "Move!" His cheeks fired red and glowing while his nostrils flared.

I reached a shaky hand toward my case. Daniel stood beside me—his hot breath washed over my skin in waves, repulsing me to my core. Time stood still, yet I could hear the ticking of the kitchen clock as though it were attached to my ear, the sound sluggish and distorted. My heart beat thundered in my chest and slammed against my ribcage.

Hoisting the suitcase to a stand, I lifted it onto the first step. I returned my gaze to Daniel's beady glare—he watched while I tried to heave my case up. My nerves steeled and my body shook. "Are you going to help me? I'm carrying your child, for God's sake." My voice rose while he continued to stare.

Daniel's mouth turned up into a gloating sneer. "You can manage. Go on." He widened his eyes and red-veined orbs bulged back at me.

He stood before me, a complete stranger who turned my life upside down, moulding me into some weak, subservient shadow of a girl. I used to be so much more than this—smart, outspoken, confident. What became of me made a mockery of the person I used to be.

"What is wrong with you?" My voice high, my fists balled around the suitcase handle. I straightened, not once taking my eyes from his.

He drove his body forward to force me back against the wall. The suitcase fell from the step and hit Daniel in the leg.

Kicking it, he screamed in my face, "You careless bitch!" before he grabbed me round the throat with enough pressure to cause my stomach to lurch, but not so much that I struggled to breath.

"What the hell has gotten into you, Daniel?" I swallowed hard past the rising bile.

"I don't have to answer to you." He spat the last part out with utter contempt. "Who the hell do you think you--"

"I'm the pregnant girlfriend you're scaring the crap out of. Who the hell do you think you are?"

With bulging eyes full of disgust he glared down at me.

"I'm sor--"

The hard slap across my face stunted the apology. I clutched my stinging cheek with one hand and glowered at him in shock. His expression remained one of cold-blooded composure.

He threw one last glance of wide-eyed hate at me then stormed out the front door—slamming it with enough force to rattle the glass in the porch.

Sliding down the wall, I crumpled into a heap on the floor, body wracked with uncontrollable sobs.

I couldn't deal with the return of his violent behaviour. The last seven months had been bliss. No punches to my arms and legs, no kicks to the ribs, no more hiding behind a locked toilet door while he calmed down and no more emergency trips to the hospital to explain away another 'fall down the stairs'. I actually thought we'd moved passed that phase when we found out about my pregnancy. I looked forward to finally settling down into a happy family life.

I couldn't go back to before. I didn't have the strength.

I needed to talk to someone.

Heading for the living room where I dropped my bag earlier, I grabbed my phone and unlocked the screen. Even though my dad would answer while he worked, I didn't want to bother him just yet.

Ever since mom died when I was a baby, my dad and I formed a very close bond. After I met Daniel our relationship changed. We loved each other just the same, but we became less reliant on one another. I guessed he figured, with me growing up, I didn't need him to protect me all the time. But I did, I just felt too ashamed to admit the daily hell I went through, until now.

Dad would be busy right now, though. He worked for the Faction—a group of vampires who policed supernatural activity in the area.

No, Alice would be better. Dad and I would need a more in-depth conversation, and being in no frame of mind to start piecing together how that would go, I typed in my best friend's number instead.

"Hey, girly, how's it going?" Alice's voice gave me comfort. "You can't be there already, surely?"

Oh wow. *Where do I start with something like this?* Tears formed and my throat constricted on any attempt to get the words to come out.

"Ellie...?"

"Sorry, I... we didn't go, he... ." The weakling in me burst into tears again.

"I'm coming right over."

Chapter 4

It took Alice fifteen minutes to get to my Mellor Brook home from her apartment in Barrow, Lancashire. Alice pulled her car onto my empty drive. I threw the door open before she could knock, and she took one wide-eyed look at my face before she paled.

"Holy shit, Ellie. What the hell happened? I'm gonna kill that no-good, motherfu--"

"Oh, Al." The reality settled in. I dropped my gaze and closed my eyes while shame washed over me. Alice pulled me into a tight embrace, rubbing a hand up and down my back while my body convulsed with laboured sobs. "This is all my fault, if I--"

"Oh hell no, this is so not your fault. Did you ask him to do this? I didn't think so." She pulled back and stared into my eyes. "He has no right to treat you this way. You're coming with me, and I don't wanna hear you argue about it, okay?" With a set face, she clutched my shoulders. "Go grab some things." Her smile softened as she rubbed my arms.

With my suitcase by the stairs, it dawned on me, I didn't know what Daniel packed. So, I shuffled upstairs,

Alice following. I grabbed a large hold-all, and removed clothes and toiletries from drawers while Alice stuffed them inside.

My body shook and sweat beaded my brow as I anticipated Daniel's return. Sickness swirled in my gut and my legs turned to lead while Alice helped me down the stairs. Stopping at the bottom she turned to me, her eyes asking the question her lips didn't need to.

"I'm ready." My words lacked conviction. *Can I do this, can I walk away?*

Alice left me little choice. With my bag in her hand, she headed out the door to her car. I followed close behind, my eyes darting about for any sign of Daniel.

*

Alice never once questioned what happened throughout the journey. When I broke down, I didn't want it to be in a car while we drove through residential areas where people might see the mess I got in.

Pulling into her allocated space, we got out and made our way up to her first-floor, two-bed apartment. She opened the door and ushered me in before setting my bag on a table in the hallway.

"Come on, let's get you a warm drink, and you can tell me what happened."

Alice led me into her huge open-plan kitchen-cum–lounge. I loved it; beautifully laid out and decorated to some very high, modern standards in creams, whites with splashes of blue here, shades of red there. Alice's parents were well off, but she worked her ass off for everything in this immaculate apartment.

I envied her in a way, with both parents to dote on her as she grew up. While I appreciated everything my dad did for me, and respected him to no end for taking on the role of Mom and Dad, it still hurt that I didn't have two parents to look after me, to correct the messes I got myself into.

I sat down on the plush cream sofa with the oversized duck-egg coloured cushions—I loved this sofa; I imagined sinking into a bank of fluffy clouds would feel much the same. Leaning my head back, I closed my eyes and listened to Alice rustling in the kitchen.

"Here you go." She placed a steaming mug of tea on the table in front of me.

"Thank you, Al. I don't know what I'd have done if you hadn't come for me."

She nodded. "What happened? Besides the obvious, I mean."

"I don't even know. He was in a foul mood all morning, but when I grabbed a few magazines at the service station he just went absolutely mental. He made a show of marching me out of the shop." I cringed at the recollection, my face heated. "I was mortified. We got into the car, and he told me to clean myself up, I opened his glove compartment, and a knife fell out, he--"

"Wait, what? What the hell's he doing with a knife in his car?"

"Well, that's what I wondered, but when I asked he went ballistic." I related to Alice the whole scary, humiliating story. Watched her eyes widen when tears rolled down my face, recalling his behaviour. I told her about what I said to him during my outburst.

"You did?" Alice smirked at my confession of a bravery I'd not shown for years. "What did he say?"

"He hit me."

"Oh, sweetie, I'm so sorry. He's a fuckin' bastard. Have you called the police?"

"Good God. No! Are you kidding me? He wouldn't like that at all."

"Who gives a shit, Ellie? He assaulted you, for crying out loud. And I *know* it's not the first time, so don't even lie to me. It's time you stood up for yourself."

The idea that Alice knew of the abuse while I hid it caused a ripple of shame to quiver through me, my eyes welled up. But the thought of going to the police about it made me feel sick. Daniel would worm his way out of it; he always did. Then I'd suffer for it.

Alice's face softened. "You can't let him get away with this anymore."

"I know," I sighed. "Let me sleep on it? This isn't going to go away in that time." I pointed at the evidence of Daniel's still-smarting assault on my face.

"Fine, but you know you have to do this. Have you called your dad?"

"No. He's at work right now. I'll go see him tomorrow."

"Good idea. And I'll come with you."

"Haven't you got work?"

"Not tomorrow, no."

"I'm sorry for dragging you into this, Al. You're a good friend. I don't deserve you."

"Hey, hush now, don't be silly." She grabbed me in a tight embrace and soothed the back of my head with her hand.

∞∞∞

Opening my eyes, I yawned and stretched before I realised Alice and I had fallen asleep on the sofa. I turned to the window—curtains still open—and noted the dark, starry sky.

Looking back, I wondered what the heck I'd do without her, my amazing, outspoken, taking-no-crap-from-anyone friend. God only knew—I'd be lost.

Alice stirred beside me. "Bloody hell, my neck doesn't half hurt now," she complained, massaging herself.

I smiled at her. "We should probably get some proper sleep. I feel exhausted, and I don't think the sofa is going to help."

"You're right, sweetheart. Let's get our arses into bed." She paused and took my hand. "Ellie, my guest room is open to you for however long you need it, okay?"

"Thanks, Al. I don't know what I'd do if you weren't in my life." My voice trembled and tears threatened to spill. Alice moved her hand from mine and put it around my shoulder.

"Hey, hey, there's no need for that, darling. I'll always be here for you, but you gotta promise to stay strong for me. You're a tough cookie, deep down. You'll be okay; I'll make sure of that, all right?"

I nodded, fighting back the tears best I could, but the odd one rolled down my cheek.

"C'mon, let's get you to bed, eh?"

With my body drained to the point of collapsing, she helped me into the guest room. I couldn't even piece together any coherent thoughts; exhausted, I needed rest. Alice, bless her soul, made sure she tucked me in before she gave me a kiss on the cheek and left the room.

Sometimes I found it hard to believe we were the same age. She knew how to handle situations better and it made her seem so much more grown up. I, on the other hand, allowed myself to be influenced into a person other than the real me.

It would stop right now.

∞ ∞ ∞

My eyes flickered open against the warm sun shining through the curtains. I touched the swell of my cheek and winced against the throbbing pain—the truth of my nightmare as real as the agony.

I lay awake and stared at the ceiling. A light knock sounded on the door and Alice walked in with a mug of steaming liquid and a small plate.

"I thought you might like some tea and toast." She placed my breakfast on the bedside table and sat down next to me. I smiled at her in thanks.

"What time you wanna go round to your dad's?"

"I'll call him first, but I'm pretty sure he doesn't work Saturdays."

"And about the other thing?"

I sighed a heavy sound; of course she wouldn't let me forget. "I'll call them after we visit Dad."

"Promise?"

Nodding, I grabbed a slice of toast and took a bite.

We spent the rest of the morning and most of the afternoon curled up on the sofa engrossed in crappy daytime TV, eating microwave pizzas—something so ordinary, so normal, yet almost alien to me. I hated Daniel even more. It felt good to feel other emotions besides fear, guilt and shame.

Calling my dad earlier that afternoon, I told him I needed to see him and so he invited me and Alice round for dinner. I stared at the empty pizza boxes and groaned—Dad cooked so much food when he expected guests; I bloated at the thought.

*

The clock read quarter to five by the time we pulled up outside Dad's house. Alice kept glancing at me during the twenty-odd-minute journey to his home in Barnoldswick. I caught a glimpse of my reflection in the wing mirror and saw why—deathly pale skin, dark circles underneath my eyes. I looked a mess; the bruises on my cheek and jaw highlighted against my pallid complexion. I didn't wear make-up; I saw little point. I preferred the natural look and only wore it after Daniel told me to make more of an effort for him.

"You ready?" Alice asked, turning to me.

Nope, but I managed a small smile and a nod before we got out of the car.

My father lived in a good-sized, Cotswold-bricked cottage which dated back to the seventeenth century. Proud of his home, an immaculate, mini-fenced in garden ran alongside the pebbled drive. It came alive with breathtaking splashes colour.

We didn't even make it all the way up the drive when the front door opened, and Daniel stood there, a smile on his face.

Chapter 5

Halting in my tracks, Alice bumped into my back.

"Ellie babe, what the...?"

Dread coursed through my veins like iced water and I shuddered. I chanced a glance at Alice to see her wide eyes locked on Daniel. The smile fell from his face when I turned my head back toward him.

"You...?" Alice's breath caught on her words.

Standing aside her, I caught a glimpse of the hate in her eyes before she launched herself at Daniel and punched him hard, in the mouth.

My mouth dropped open and my eyes widened. I caught Daniel's look of similar surprise. It seemed neither of us expected her attack. Nevertheless, my body shook in anticipation of his reaction.

Daniel stumbled back. I cringed at the sight of him. He stared straight through Alice as though she were nothing to him. He glared at me with such loathing, and the corners of his mouth turned up into a sly smirk.

"Alice Watkins, what on earth do you think you're playing at?" My dad's voice boomed from somewhere in the hallway.

Daniel's features softened; his act of airs and graces fell back into place.

"What is this psychotic bastard doing here, Bernie?" Alice shouted back, Daniel's six foot one frame blocking most of her view.

My dad moved from behind him and, though an inch or two shorter, placed a firm hand on Daniel's arm. Seconds away from leading him back inside he looked over at me. It took a moment for his grey brow to furrow, then his eyes widened and his face paled. Shame and embarrassment gripped me; my legs went weak and threatened to give way.

"Elora, sweetheart, are you okay? What happened to you?" His voice came out a choked whisper as he moved toward me, his glassy eyes roaming my cheek and jaw.

"Why don't you ask this piece of rectal scum?" Alice shoved Daniel in the arm, but he didn't retaliate, he just glared at her with a fire in his eyes, daring her to touch him again.

Dad stood before me and placed a gentle hand to my face. I winced.

"Did he do this?" He turned to Daniel, running one hand through his shock of silver hair, the other remained on my cheek. "Did you do this?"

"Of course I didn't! Why on earth would I hurt her? I love her." He switched his gaze to me, fury buried behind his stare. "Why are you doing this, Ellie? I was so scared when I got back yesterday and you weren't there."

My mouth fell open at the crap spewing from his. I trembled beneath my dad's touch and my anger surged. "Is that why you neglected to call me? You were so worried, yet you never phoned me to find out where I was? Stop doing this, Daniel. I've put up with it for far too long."

His nostrils flared at my response and his eyes flashed angry surprise. "I thought you needed some space. You looked so upset when I had to cancel our holiday because of work. I know how much you'd been looking forward to it, and I said I was sorry."

How dare you? My eyes bulged while my rage spiked. "Work? You cancelled our holiday because of work? So it had nothing to do with the knife I found in your car?"

"Knife?" my dad exclaimed. He looked between Daniel and me.

"Mr. Lincoln, there was no such thing." Daniel threw me a quick glare and his chest eased out a heavy breath before he turned back to my dad. "Elora's just been really tired lately. The baby's been causing her a bit of stress and keeping her awake at night. She's started to see things that aren't there--"

"No! No more!" The outburst startled everyone, me in particular, since it exploded from my mouth. "You are not going to ruin my life any longer, you sick, twisted psychopath." I turned to my dad, eyes pleading. "Yes, I did find a knife in his car and, yes, he did this to me because I questioned him over it. It isn't the first time he's laid a finger on me, either."

Voice raised, I stood firm, defiant, and stared back at Daniel. My chest heaved with each laboured breath.

His lip twitched. "Ellie, darling, you're not yourself right now. The stress with the baby being due soon, it's scrambled your fragile mind."

"Don't you dare talk to my daughter like that. The only thing that would possibly be fragile about her mind is whatever mess you've obviously caused in there. If you come anywhere near her again, I'll put you six feet under, do you understand me?" My father's eruption shocked me, quite like mine a minute ago.

Daniel's face darkened and he took a few menacing steps toward my dad, lips drawn back, he looked... evil. He squared up to my dad, and I shrank away from their standoff.

"Listen to me, old man, and listen good. That child inside of *your* daughter belongs to *me!* We will be back for it the moment it's born, and there won't be a damn thing you can do to stop us. Do *you* understand *me?*" Daniel's thundering voice sent chills down my spine, even Dad and Alice paled.

But he could go to hell talking to him like that.

"Back off, Daniel," I spat at him through clenched teeth.

I moved closer and chanced a glimpse at Alice's look of surprise, her face mimicking her red hair as she talked into her phone—to the police, I assumed.

"Shall I share something with you, Bernie?" Ignoring my eruption, Daniel's tone lowered, his eyes dark, almost black, retaining his otherworldly look. "That daughter of yours is one fine lay. She's so juicy and tight. I'm going to miss her when that baby is born."

Oh hell no! A red mist descended. Fury rippled through me with a strength and resolve I never knew I possessed. Rage swirled in my belly and heat seared a scorching trail through my blood. My skin burned and my fingertips prickled.

I reached for Daniel's shoulder. "Get away from us!" I screamed. A static charge jumped from him to me and I shook out the tingle in my fingers.

Daniel turned to face me, surprise in his wide eyes before his face turned ashen. My dad grabbed hold of Daniel's shoulder and kneed him in the genitals.

Doubling over, Daniel's face turned an ugly shade of reddish purple. An immense, thriving energy somersaulted around my stomach and bounced off every inch of my buzzing body.

Daniel's expression changed to something far more sinister, and a threatening smile crinkled his squinted eyes. "You're both going to regret this moment for as long as you live."

"The police should be here any minute," Alice announced, loud enough for us all to hear.

Daniel turned and ran down the street. An engine gunned and he raced passed us in his car, amid screeching tires and the acrid stench of burnt rubber.

Alice ran over to me. "Are you okay? Jesus Christ, that guy is a nutcase. What the hell did he mean when he said 'we will be back'? Who the hell is 'we'?"

Realisation dawned, and I cradled my belly—he *did* say "we," and "there won't be a damn thing you can do to stop *us*." With light-headedness, my body slumped into Alice's and Dad's firm hold.

∞ ∞ ∞

I gave the police my statement about Daniel's ongoing abuse—I left nothing out. While the experience proved difficult to relive, I couldn't fault the attitude of the two officers who interviewed me; they didn't pressure me, just asked questions, took photos and wrote notes. With promises to be in touch, they left me with some counselling leaflets.

Drained by the end of it, my appetite for dinner subsided. Outside, seated on a patio chair, I indulged in what remained of the warm, evening sun. I reflected on what all this meant for me—for us—while I caressed my bump. No way would I let Daniel get his hands on my child—the police would also help see to that.

Looking down at the half-eaten salad on the table in front of me, I started to pick at it again when my dad came out of the cottage.

"Elora, the police just called."

The officers who took my statement told me they planned to go round to my home in search of Daniel.

Home.

My hand stilled over my plate as I contemplated that word.

Did it ever feel like home?

I thought so, once upon a time. I kept it clean, cooked his meals, played the doting housewife. I'd been proud.

But Daniel chose the décor, decided which room would be which, where the furniture went, he picked the curtains, the dining set, the bed. Him, him, him.

A heat flared inside me. It had been his castle, and I his slave. His domain.

Well, he could fucking have it for all I cared. I didn't want to live in a place reeking of his very essence—where his influence poured from every furnishing, wall and floor.

"Elora?"

I apologised to my father and recalled his statement. "That was quick."

I didn't like the look on my dad's face at all—his ice blue eyes held a sadness beneath half-raised brows.

"He wasn't at home. Neither was his car. They think he's done a runner, sweetheart."

I went cold despite the sun's heat. My stomach sank while I fought against the urge to be sick. My voice trembled, "He'll come after me and my baby."

Kneeling in front of me, Dad placed two reassuring hands on my legs. "No, he won't, angel. I'm not letting you out of my sight."

"That's impossible, Dad. You have to work."

"I've called the Faction and they're making up some rooms for us."

"Oh, Dad, don't be daft. That's too drastic."

"I don't care, darling. That psycho threatened to take your baby, not to mention the hints that there are others involved in... well, whatever he's involved in."

The reminder shook me to the core and brought with it fresh bouts of nausea. "Dad... how am I meant to live in a building run by vampires?"

My dad looked taken aback by my question. "They won't hurt you."

I chuckled, "No, Dad. What I meant is how do I adjust? Don't they just come out at night?"

He laughed at me—a glorious sound, "Oh, sweetheart, no. They can't go in direct sunlight, or they'll burn, but they do work during the day. The Compound can be closed off from sunlight."

"How claustrophobic."

"They have a couple of huge gardens you can get a breath of fresh air in. They also have modern guest quarters, a library, a huge fully staffed kitchen, a hospital wing, and a full security team. You'll be fine, and perfectly safe."

It still sounded oppressive to me—I could imagine being bored out of my mind without much to do there. But it didn't matter—the safety of my child trumped all else. And, at the end of the day, I didn't want to be away from my dad right now—Daniel would come for us. He said as much. At least guarded by vampire warriors, we would be safe from him, and whoever *they* were.

∞ ∞ ∞

Pulling up outside the Compound in Marles Wood, I grabbed the case of my belongings Alice went back to her apartment for, before she headed to work.

In the velvety darkness the Compound stood, a grand edifice against the backdrop of dense woodland; a modern structure surrounded by walls twenty feet high, topped with another two foot of barbed wire. Floodlights bathed the entire yard in a bright, white glare. Two guard towers stood either side of two sets of thick, barred gates, and two more behind those.

Dad told me human patrol units manned the entire Compound, and the barbed wire on top of the walls could be electrified at the push of a button.

Being here for the first time, it left a weird, nervous feeling in the pit of my stomach.

Taking my bag off me, Dad shouldered his and motioned for me to follow. We stood before the thick steel gates and Dad pulled his ID out. He swiped it over a security mechanism on the wall. After that, he bent down to a monitor for a retina scan and, after attaching heartbeat sensors to his chest and head, submitted his thumb to the pad for a fingerprint scan.

"Wow, bit security conscious?" I commented, standing beside him. My voice trembled.

I gawked at the Compound, unsure whether I felt safe or scared. *Have I thought this through?* Vampires. I would be living with creatures of the night who fed on fresh blood.

Sure, my dad *said* they weren't the blood-thirsty savages of centuries-old tales, but how could *I* be certain of that?

"They have to be, flower. Amongst other reasons, there are a lot of ancient relics in this building that could be lethal in the wrong hands."

"Oh."

I caressed my swollen belly and swallowed past the lump in my throat. *What choice do I have?* The Faction *may not* want to feed on me or my unborn child, but Daniel *did* want us, and his intentions would be less than amiable.

My dad had worked for the Faction for five years—they'd never once hurt him. I needed to do this. For my baby's sake, if not for my own.

The first set of gates buzzed open and we walked into a small area between them. We waited for the first set to close before the second set opened. Once through, we made our way to the front of the building. The impressive entrance before me stood huge, with a large windowed façade that I could only see my reflection in.

Swiping his ID card once more, Dad took a small step back before the glass-fronted doors opened into a sleek reception area.

Black marble tiles adorned the floors, walls painted in contrasting greys and whites. Several glass-topped coffee tables lined one end with plush, grey sofas set around them. Green potted plants added a splash of colour and the subdued lighting created a calming atmosphere.

The cool, open air filled my lungs and the sweet aroma of lilies and honeysuckle tickled my senses. I closed my eyes and smiled as my fears began to subside.

"Evening, Wendy."

I opened my eyes at my dad's voice and noted a large desk at the far end of the reception. A woman sat behind it amid a bank of computers, keypads and telephones.

She beamed at my father. "Evening, B. This must be your lovely daughter."

"In the flesh," he smiled.

Everyone who knew my dad called him B—short for Bernie, which is short for Bernard, but no-one called him that.

Getting up from her chair, Wendy walked round to the front of the counter. A somewhat large lady with a wide, infectious grin, dark hair scrunched in a bun and red rosy cheeks. She gave me a wide smile, but her eyes threw a quick glance to the bruise on my cheek. I dropped my gaze, but she grabbed my hand and held it between her two.

"Hi, Elora, my name's Wendy. It's really nice to meet you. Your dad talks about you a lot."

"He does?" I turned to Dad and he winked at me.

"Oh yes. Worships the ground you walk on, he does."

I liked Wendy—cheerful, pleasant and she made me smile like a fool, despite my situation.

"And this must be the precious little girly." Wendy placed chubby, warm hands on my bump.

Facing life as a single mother didn't fill me with great confidence—would I be judged? Where would people assume the father was? Would they pity me because of the bruises on my face? Question after question sent me light-headed and nauseous, but Wendy's gaze showed no judgement as she grinned between me and my belly.

"That's my bun. Weeks away from joining us," I returned with a half-smile.

"Oh, I bet you are so excited! Have you thought of any names yet?"

"No, not really." In truth, Daniel suggested we not pick any names because we'd know her name the moment we laid eyes on her.

Against his wishes—but not to his knowledge—I chose a couple I liked the sound of. With him out of the picture now, it left an empty feeling inside the pit of my stomach. My child would be fatherless in essence. Yet, I would be free. We both would. But it still didn't stop the speculation and the 'what ifs'.

Wendy returned to her computers and buzzed us into an elevator. Dad swiped his key card again and we ascended.

Entering a large foyer-type area with bannisters overlooking the reception below, we headed through a set of double doors in front of us and moved into a vast sitting space. The floor went down a level where large, interlinked sofas surrounded a huge square fireplace in the middle of the room—the suspended flume went up into the ceiling. I marvelled at the beauty of the fire; watching it glow an unusual blue.

Windows lined some of the walls, and thick blackout blinds were rolled up to expose the gorgeous gardens and the beautiful moonlit Lancashire countryside below. Spotlights fixed into the ceiling produced a warm ambience, and I could hear the delicate sounds of a harp accompanied by the soft tones of a piano in the background.

Looking further into the room, I noticed a few closed doors on a couple of the walls, and a bar set in the far corner.

"This place is impressive," My fears of claustrophobia sailed away with the idyllic soundscape floating through the air.

"And this is only the main lounge. You wait 'til you see the rest of the place."

Before Dad and I could make a move toward the sofas, one of the doors opened and a man walked out, his attention buried in the paperwork he carried. His nose twitched, and he looked up.

Wow! Words failed me when his gaze slammed into mine with the powerful force of a tsunami. I stared into a set of the most piercing, beautiful eyes—a deep, glistening purple. They accentuated his short, chocolate-brown hair, light stubble, and a perfectly defined face set atop muscled flawlessness.

The fitted, short-sleeved white shirt he wore, with the top two buttons undone clung to a toned chest and abs in such a way my stomach fluttered into my throat. His strong, brawny arms covered in tattoos, and his tight in-all-the-right-places, black jeans… they were made for him.

I could feel my heartbeat as it pounded; threatening to burst out of my chest with the way his gazed ensnared me.

A nagging little noise in my left ear jilted my concentration, and I realised my dad had been trying to get my attention.

"Ellie, are you okay?"

I blinked a couple of times and shook my head. "Um… yeah, thanks."

The newcomer acknowledged my dad's presence with a quick nod.

I turned my gaze back to the vampire Adonis, who came to stand before me. His natural speed made him lightning fast.

He took a gentle hold of my hand and placed his lips to it, "Miss Lincoln, my name is Deacon De Luca. It's nice to finally put a face to the name."

I heated as his soft, pink lips brushed against the skin on the back of my hand. The friction sent electricity surging through my whole body at his slightest touch. If he felt it, too, he didn't show it, but he did look me in the eyes when he spoke to me.

"Please, call me Elora." I forced the words out.

"Elora….." He let my name linger while he stared at me.

In that instant, as my name escaped his lips and my stomach fluttered, I *knew* my life would never be the same.

∞∞∞

Having gone to the labs to work, Dad left me in Deacon's company.

Dad talked about Deacon to me before; I knew him to be a four-hundred year old member of the Faction—and, damn, he looked good for his age.

Arms linked, he gave me a tour of the library and media rooms before we ended in the large kitchen/dining area. I didn't register much of the black and white marble surroundings, instead I hung off Deacon's every word, committed the feel of his cool skin on mine to memory. I tried to focus on the rooms he showed me, but when he gazed into my eyes, held my stare, I lost all concentration.

My earlier reservations over staying here slipped away with each word he breathed. We would be safe here—my baby and I.

I didn't feel uncomfortable around Deacon, either. Only delightful bliss. And I wondered why.

"This place is magnificent," I exclaimed, breaking eye contact in an attempt to mask my infatuation.

I caught Deacon's smile before he, too, turned away. "It's certainly something. Can I make you anything to eat or drink?"

I shook my head. "I'm not hungry, but thank you."

He placed a gentle hand on my arm and looked me in the eye before he uttered, "Ellie, I promised your dad I'd make sure you ate something."

Oh my—my legs quivered at the way he breathed my nickname as if it were intended for his lips only. His voice wrapped around me like silk and sent shivers down my spine. My body tuned in to its femininity, begging me to throw myself at the sexual mercy of this beautiful man.

What the hell is wrong with me? He's offering food, not a lifetime commitment. "I guess I could eat a sandwich or something, if you're sure you don't mind."

"It'd be my pleasure, Elora." *Wow*, his words rolled off his tongue like liquid gold—the way he whispered my name left me wet and throbbing and I didn't even care to know why he affected me this way. I wanted to revel in a sensation I'd not felt in a long time.

Closing my eyes, I took a deep breath and released it while those familiar stirrings stroked my body over and over.

"Are you feeling okay? You're breathing rather heavily, and you're glowing." Deacon's voice sailed into my ears on silver-lined clouds—so beautiful and full of genuine concern, with a hint of... *what was that...?*

... Jesus H. Christ, can he sense what I'm feeling? I suppressed a groan at the thought.

I turned to face him to tell him I felt fine—I didn't, of course, but I couldn't let him know. Opening my mouth to speak, in a flash, he appeared in front of me. He traced his hand around the bruise on my face with a feather-light touch. I closed my eyes and committed his gentle caress to memory while my skin heated and puckered under his soft fingers.

My body groaned at me, pulled at some hidden, charged connection—something so deep I didn't understand it, but so powerful I couldn't ignore it.

"I will never understand how a man can harm a precious woman."

His words took me by surprise and my eyes snapped open.

His lips curled up and I blushed at his smile. Heat seared my skin when his boyish smirk caused dimples in his cheeks. My knees weakened. Already, this man did things to me he didn't even realise, and he only touched my face.

He drew back, a look of regret across his features as his brows dipped. "I'm so sorry, I shouldn't have--"

"It's okay." I squeezed out, and my heart sank a little.

I looked into his eyes. *Kiss me, kiss me right now.*

"Ahem." Someone to the right of me cleared his throat with excessive exaggeration.

Peeling my gaze away from Deacon's to stare at my new-found enemy, I choked on my words.

Wow, seriously? Were all these vampire guys hot? This one stood a hair taller than Deacon, but with a similar build. He sported an "Ivy league" blond haircut, and the same purple eyes. His face held a boyish charm, with a chiselled jaw and a dimple in his chin.

"Keeping her all to yourself, Deak?" the newcomer laughed when he glanced in Deacon's direction. He looked back at me. "What's your name, pretty lady?"

"Elora," I murmured.

He looked to my bump with a smile as he walked toward me, and grabbed my small hand in his large one. "I'm Blake Bennett, and boy, does my bro work fast."

"Behave yourself, Blake. This is B's daughter." Deacon growled.

"No kidding? Your pictures don't do you justice." Blake stared at me with a lopsided smile.

I blushed.

Returning his stare to Deacon, he told him, "Sorry to break up the party, but we're needed in conference room one."

Deacon nodded. "I'll show Ellie to her room, and then I'll be right in."

Blake smirked. "Take your time, dude." He turned to me and winked. "Nice to meet you… Ellie." With one final grin at Deacon, he left.

"Sorry about him. He's an insufferable ass." Deacon rolled his eyes.

I giggled before he went about whipping me up a cheese sandwich and a glass of juice. "C'mon, I'll show you where you'll be staying."

*

Deacon led me around a maze of corridors to a breath-taking room. It housed one large window at the back, a king-size bed positioned in front of it. The bed frame itself, crafted from a light oak, stood on a raised platform with two steps leading up. To either side of it, two bedside tables with lamps, the lamp bases made from a tarnished metal sculpted into amalgamations of lovers in different erotic embraces.

To one side of the room stood a double-sized wardrobe made from the same warm, wood as the bed frame and tables. A large, white, shag pile rug lay in front of the dais accommodating the bed—it contrasted well with the cream carpet present throughout. On the other side of the room, a good sized, cream-coloured sofa with large, luxurious, chocolate and burgundy cushions—in front of this a flat screen TV, also of ample size, and to the left of the TV, the door to the en-suite.

I strode to the window—at least two storeys high and facing the back of the property. Along with the calming ambience of my room, the high walls and electrified fences atop them put me at ease.

"You should find it comfortable enough…." Deacon seemed to hesitate, "If it isn't too late when I get done, can I come by and see you later?"

Oh my, long forgotten memories of butterflies flapped around my stomach, and I struggled to put together an intelligible answer for fear they'd escape through my mouth. I nodded and smiled.

Smiling back, Deacon moved to plant a soft, lasting kiss on my cheek.

I closed my eyes and savoured the sensations coursing through me, sparking fires in all the right places. Aches and throbs caused me to grip his bicep and I groaned against his touch. When I opened my eyes, Deacon disappeared, but I could still smell his sweet, honey scent lingering in the hallway.

Chapter 6

Bonded

An electrifying connection with another being so unbreakable, so potent it couldn't be ignored. A magnetic pull from which one couldn't explain nor hide.

A vampire could live a thousand years and never find that person with which life truly began. Never experience that crashing desire to offer them your very soul just for one touch, one kiss. To meet your eternal mate ignited you from the inside; an all-consuming *need* to be there, to protect, love, die for that person.

Elora is that person. I am hers, as she is mine.

Her decadent flavour coated Deacon's lips. His very being ached to be near such an exquisite, pure creature. When their eyes first met, mere hours ago, Deacon knew his destiny meant belonging to her—mind, body and soul.

A dynamic strength erupted from within him, an ethereal connection poured from his body and entwined with hers; with her beauty, her strength, her spirit.

His senses heightened and the drumming of her heart against her chest etched an everlasting, feverish beat on the very substance of his existence.

Her taste lingered while he made his way to the conference room, and he walked in beaming from ear to ear.

"Got it bad, don't ya, buddy?" Blake's cocky grin met him from across the room.

"Shut it, Blake. Where's Lucas?" He hid his smile, *time to get my game-face back on.*

"Ooh, touchy." Blake's smirk spread wider. "He's gone to fetch those coppers that are meant to be working with us."

Deacon wasn't slow to miss the note of disparagement in Blake's low, whiny voice.

"Of course. You haven't worked with Amelia and her team yet, have you?"

"I don't see why we have to involve the local plod in a supernatural case."

"Because witches are human, Blake, you know this. Besides, Amelia is an asset where witches are involved. She knows her stuff."

Blake shrugged his shoulders and crossed his arms. He averted his eyes and pouted like a child placed in the middle of a sweet shop and told not to touch anything.

Moments later, the door to the meeting room opened, and Lucas walked in, followed by Amelia.

Blake looked up. His eyes flashed wide and his mouth parted. "Wow," he breathed.

Deacon smirked and turned to the dark-blonde haired DCI as she shifted from foot to foot, uncomfortable. Blake continued to stare, devouring her with unblinking eyes.

"Amelia, this is Blake," Lucas introduced them.

In the past, the paranormal cases Amelia worked on didn't amount to a murder so grave. The Compound deemed Deacon and Nate enough manpower to manage the small workloads. Clearly, having a stranger gawk at her like a prime piece of steak didn't sit too comfortably with her.

She opened her mouth, "Wha--"

"Amelia and her guys were at the crime scene with Nate this morning, and came across something quite grim." Lucas placed his hands on the hefty table before him.

Shifting his gaze to Lucas, Blake's expression remained wide-eyed, but changed to something of wonderment as his brow arched. "What do you mean, General?"

"We'll wait for Nate to arrive, then we'll get started."

Sitting his large frame at the grey stone table, Lucas ran a hand through thick, brown hair, before he motioned for Amelia to take a seat with the others. The DCI sat opposite Blake, eyeing him while she lowered herself, his stare, once again, fixed on her.

Nate bounded through the door, trying to balance several large, ancient-looking tomes in his arms.

"What the hell, man? I hope you ain't expecting us to read all of that," Blake wagged an accusatory finger at Nate as he stole his attention from Amelia for a brief second.

"You can read?" came Nate's sarcastic response before he slammed the books onto the table. "Who knew?"

Blake scowled. "Your mum sa--"

"What are these for, Nate?" Lucas interjected.

"After uncovering some evidence at the crime scene, we did some research. We connected the stuff we found; baby taken, sacrificial knife fragments, owl's claw. Now, correct me if I'm wrong, but this all points to an attempt to resurrect--"

"Lilith!" Lucas finished, his back straightening while his eyes bore into Nate's.

"Yeah, we're in no doubt about it. Look here....." Amelia grabbed one of the books from Nate's pile and opened it to a page they'd obviously marked earlier. They stared at the familiar cross and crescent moon symbol. "This was scrawled on the wall in the victim's blood. It's the symbol of Lilith."

"What are all these books?" Blake directed his intense gaze at her.

Amelia took a deep breath. "Different versions of the Bible, depending on which religion you look at. Lilith is mentioned in most ancient texts, but descriptions of her differ, as do some of the less important myths. But there are things that remain the same."

"Such as?" Lucas question forced her eyes away from Blake.

"Lilith was Adam's first wife, before Eve. According to texts, she was the first female to be cast out of Heaven following the Great Heavenly War. She became Adam's mate, but refused to submit to him as a lesser being. She wanted equality, Adam denied it to her, and so she sprouted black wings and fled the Garden of Eden.

"Being a demon of passion, instinct, and desire, she fornicated with numerous demons and produced evil offspring. Three angels were sent to take her back to Adam, but when she refused, they killed all of her children--"

Blake scoffed and Amelia glared at him. "Problem?"

"Intriguing as it all sounds, why are witches sacrificing babies to raise her, and why now?"

"I was getting to that," she responded, releasing a breath. She averted her eyes and addressed the group once more. "As a result of the murder of her children, she vowed to slay any child that did not bear the name of these angels on an amulet around his or her neck. Our best guess is that they're taking the lives of babies just as she did.

"I couldn't tell you exactly why the witches feel the need to raise Lilith now, but I can tell you it will have something to do with a man. Lilith resented her position as Adam's inferior, and so she continued to produce offspring known as Lilium, who would seduce men and often kill them. We think at least one of these witches has been wronged and are attempting to raise Lilith so that she can produce her Lilium to wipe--"

"One small problem with that, Dollface," Blake began, "how's Lilith gonna get knocked up without her demons at hand?"

Amelia let out a prolonged breath and tensed her jaw. Placing her hands on the table, she glared at Blake. "Listen, arsehole, if you interrupt me once more, I'm gonna ram this Bible so far up your arse you'll be reciting scriptures for a month."

Nate stifled a laugh and attempted to cover it up with an exaggerated cough. Blake shot him a dirty, squinted look.

Amelia smirked and carried on, "Keep quiet for a few minutes, and I can tell you that Lilith can impregnate herself through masturbation or erotic dreams. She can do the same for others."

"Sexy," Blake grinned.

Amelia raised her eyebrows, the shadow of a smile creeping through.

"So, they're after revenge?" Deacon intervened, his lack of contribution a consequence of his thoughts filtering between the case, and the sweet look on Elora's porcelain-smooth face before he left her in her room.

"It looks that way," Amelia nodded, "but I don't think they have any idea what they're attempting to unleash."

"So, why not just take revenge a different way? Kill, maim, cast some spell that gives these men genital herpes for the rest of their lives?" This time, Blake made a good point.

"Good question, but I don't know. That's what we need to figure out," Slight resignation filtered through Amelia's words and her shoulders dropped. "Nate, didn't you say there'd be more?" she reminded.

Nate nodded. "It depends how many disciples the coven leader managed to convince to do her bidding. She won't be acting alone."

"So, the head witch will be the one wronged then?" Deacon's gaze wandered around the room and rested back on Nate.

"Seems so, yeah," Nate nodded again.

"Is there any way to figure out the next target?" The group met Amelia's question with a deafening silence.

∽∽∽

Amelia remained at the Compound after sending Sam and Chloe home to study their gathered information.

The exhausted DCI needed to find any motives or clues to suggest who the next victim, or victims, might be. She opted to stay behind to use the vast archives in the hopes she could try and shed some light on their predicament.

The door opened as she stifled a yawn, and Blake walked in.

"You should get some rest," he offered.

"I'm fine. I'll sleep when the job's complete," she answered in a weary drone, flexing her neck before she massaged the ache settled there.

"Suit yourself. I've been in the labs analysing the residue you found on the victim's ankles and wrists.

"And...?"

"Results aren't back yet."

"Something else you wanted, then?"

"I'm sorry if I upset you earlier."

His unexpected apology made her eyes shoot to his. "You are?"

"I got too far ahead of myself. I can be an arse like that, sometimes."

"Sometimes?" Amelia's lips hitched into a smirk.

Blake's reciprocated smile looked sheepish. "Okay, I guess I deserved that."

"Yes, you did." Amelia looked back down at the book in front of her.

"Found anything else, yet?" Blake asked, his voice expectant.

She shook her head. "Not really, no. I'm trying to find any mention that anyone has ever attempted this before--"

"Of course witches have attempted to raise demons before."

Amelia cocked her eyebrow at him.

Blake ran an imaginary zipper across his lips.

"I meant Lilith in particular, she's not exactly a demon in the original sense," she continued.

"What do you mean?" His brow hitched and he strode over to sit in one of leather chairs opposite her.

Amelia turned the book towards him. "Demons are angels that rebelled against God and followed Satan when he was cast out. They're known as Fallen Angels. Lilith was the first human female on earth created by God, but not *from* man, as Eve was. When she was cast out, she wasn't made into a Fallen Angel *because* she was human, not an angel to begin with. She goes above and beyond what would create the usual demons. Her actions led her down her own path, and she became something entirely different and, get this, apparently she could shift into the form of an owl."

"Explains the claw. Is there anything in there about how she died, or how to kill her?"

"Nope. There's not even anything that gives credibility to the stories of her existence. She isn't acknowledged at all in some of these texts, so for all we know, this could all be just myth. One story does say that, once she left Adam, God created Eve from one of Adam's ribs as Lilith became the first vampire, known as the Queen of the Demons."

Blake scoffed. "I think we'd know about her if she were related to our kin in any way."

"There are so many conflicting stories about who she actually was; demon, witch, vampire. It's about as implausible as the existence of the Greek or Roman Gods. People believe what they want to believe for their own security and reasoning, but it doesn't necessarily make it fact."

"But the witches believe it?"

"Yes, they do. And they're committing murder in the name of their beliefs."

Amelia and Blake studied texts until the early hours of the morning, but couldn't find much more to help them figure out what the witches planned next.

Amelia yawned for the umpteenth time that night.

"You really do need to get some rest. You're more than welcome to stay here in our guest quarters," Blake's stomach fluttered in the hope she would accept his invitation.

Frenzied want soared when he gazed into her heavy-lidded, hazel eyes and he struggled against his desire to close his eyes and inhale the succulent scent emanating from her delectable body.

An impassioned fire danced deep in his core and his entire being pined for this woman. *His* woman.

Women, for the most part, threw themselves at him, he could have his pick. For Amelia to spurn his advances, resist his charms, only strengthened his want for her.

"I should get back home."

Blake's heart sank with her words, but they didn't deter him. "You shouldn't drive when you're tired. You could have an accident and injure that pretty little face of yours."

"I didn't know you cared." Amelia reddened, but held his stare.

"I don't," he shrugged, "but I don't want your death on my conscience when you could've stayed here."

She placed her hands on the table in front of her and leaned in. "You'd better show me to a room, then." Raising a brow, she threw him a half-curved smile.

A jolt from his seat sent Blake's chair crashing to the ground. With a wide grin, he held his hand out for the smirking DCI, and led her out the library, through a maze of corridors.

He paused outside a door, positioned his hand on the wall in front of her and leaned in close.

"Need me to help tuck you in?" He winked at her.

"What makes you think I can't see to it myself?" She parted her mouth and dashed her tongue across her top lip in an effort to hide her discernible smile.

"Oh, I'm pretty certain you have no problems *seeing* to yourself, just thought I'd do the polite thing and offer."

Amelia sucked her bottom lip between her teeth and flared her nostrils. Ducking under his arm, she opened the door a fraction, a wavering breath escaping her body.

She peered over her shoulder. "I'll see you later, Ace, but for tonight I think I'll take care of things on my own." She turned around and looked into his eyes with a smirk, while she closed the door.

Ace? Where the hell did that come from? He liked it.

Blake's erection pressed painfully against his trousers. *Christ, she is hot. That body, those eyes.* And Ace?

This woman would be his.

Chapter 7

A loud knock at the door caused Amelia to jump out of bed. *Jesus Christ, who the hell is banging at this time?* She looked at her alarm clock—4:42am.

"You've got to be kidding me," she moaned aloud.

She stumbled to the door, bleary eyed and on shaky legs. "This had better be bloody important," she murmured with clear agitation, throwing the door open.

"Dreaming about me, were you?"

She snapped her head up and met Blake's deep gaze—desire poured from his hooded expression in thick waves.

"What do you want, Blake?" She pulled the shirt she wore tight across her breasts, aware her long legs were still on display.

"Well, now there's a loaded question." Blake's focus drank her in from head to toe and he licked his curved lips.

In spite of herself, Amelia smiled. "Seriously, what the hell?"

Blake dropped the smile. "There's been another one."

∾∾∾

Given the hour, neither Deacon nor Blake could accompany Amelia to the crime scene, but Nate arrived on location, and she called Sam and Chloe to meet her back at the Compound in a few hours.

Another warehouse, another murder.

"Good morning, Inspector," Nate offered her a half-smile from the window of his rusted, old van.

Amelia left her car to lean on the doorframe of Nate's deathtrap. "Been here long?"

"Long enough. Care to take a look?"

"Might as well," Amelia stepped away from the door so Nate could exit the van. "Same as before?"

"Pretty much."

"Did you find any evidence of a perp from the last scene? Any fingerprints, fibres, hairs?"

"Actually, yes. I did pick up a few black hairs, but nothing matched in any databases. I've got Sebastian working on it."

Sebastian Barrow, the Faction's lab technician, could work wonders with even the tiniest bit of evidence—Amelia wondered how he would be getting on with this case, though.

"But we're still no closer to an ID?" Amelia inferred.

"Not yet. We're putting the feelers out there among the supernatural community, but so far no one's come forward."

"Once this is over, remind me to create some kind of paranormal DNA database for you guys," Amelia smiled and shook her head.

"Wouldn't be a bad idea, in all honesty," Nate smirked back.

Amelia rolled her eyes—no way did she have the patience to even attempt to *try* and catalogue the profiles for the multitude of supernaturals in existence, even if it were possible.

Inside another derelict warehouse, another crime scene, the smell hit Amelia square in the face.

"Jesus! I can see how you managed to sniff this one out."

"Yeah, from a few miles away."

This warehouse contained no extended room—the body lay in the furthest corner of the building amid the familiar sight of candles and blood. Amelia didn't hesitate and strolled over, kit in one hand, torch in the other.

Flicking her light on, she crouched down. "Same incisions," she observed, sweeping the beam across the victim's stomach.

Nate took the camera wrapped around his neck and snapped off a few pictures of the scene.

"Look at this." He motioned for Amelia to join him near the far wall. "What do you make of that?"

Amelia got up close and inspected the familiar symbol of Lilith burnt into the wall, dried blood flaked around it... *wait...*.

Upon closer inspection, she explained, "Lilith's symbol is the one in blood, not burnt into the wall. It's covering something else. Do you think they tried to hide it with Lilith's?"

"Hardly. If Lilith's symbol is in blood, then whatever was burning beneath it isn't evident anymore; there's nothing left to conceal." Nate looked perplexed. "What would a witch be burning a wall for?"

Fumbling in her kit she told Nate, "I think I know." She used the swab from her bag to dab at the smouldering remains, careful to miss the blood.

Walking back to the butchered body lay sprawled across the floor, she dug out another cotton bud and swabbed around wrists in the same position and state as the last victim.

"What you got, Millie?"

"It'll still need to be tested in the labs, but look at this…," Amelia held both swabs up against the dim candlelight and showed them to Nate while he squatted down beside her. "It's the same stuff."

The residue on both swabs continued to smoulder, an unusual orange-brown against the white cotton. With a deep sniff of each, the foul odour of decayed flesh and sulphur clawed at the back of her throat.

Amelia waved them in front of Nate.

"They're the same, but what does it mean?" Nate stood, wafting the stench away with his hand.

"It means that these witches have been controlling lesser demons. They've been summoning them through a portal they burned into the wall. The demons hold their victims down while their babies are cut from the stomach. Once their job is done, they disappear back into the portal, which closes behind them; like a secret door. It burns out and leaves behind the stench of the souls decomposing in--"

"Holy Hell."

"Well, you're half right."

"Have you seen something like this before, then?"

Amelia nodded, her jaw rigid. "A couple of times. A witch's summoning gone wrong."

"And the results?" Nate furrowed his brow.

"Horrific." Amelia glanced back down at the mutilated body. "Come on, let's finish up here and get her back to the lab. Sebastian might be able to tell us more."

∞∞∞

I stood in a pitch black room. How did I get here? *An awful stench clawed its way to the back of my throat and clung to my taste buds. It tasted of rot and decay, and I swallowed a few times to stop myself being sick.*

It took long moments for my eyesight to adjust to the pitch black, but then lights began to flare up one at a time around me, rising at least six inches high. They were surrounded by salt.

Looking around the room, I made out a bundle of red rags. Blood red rags!

My body began to tremble, and I broke out into a cold sweat, my breathing erratic. Despite my bad feeling about this, I couldn't stop myself. I inched closer toward the tattered heap on the floor.

The stench became stronger the closer I got. I stilled, hearing whispers from nowhere in particular. I wanted to throw my hands against my ears and scream to drown out the ever-increasing sounds. They changed to harsh, rasping words I couldn't discern. Panicked. Desperate.

Lily? Were they saying Lily?

With my hands over my ears, I edged closer to what I now noted to be two bodies, immobile and saturated in deep red crimson. After the final few steps, bile rose in my throat.

Staring into the dead, glassy eyes of two women, I tried to scream. No sound escaped my lips, but my throat burned raw from the effort.

Blood-caked hair swathed their gaunt, skeletal faces and their stomachs gaped open, sliced with careless abandon from throat to groin. Slick, red gore congealed across the walls and floors. It seeped towards me, slow and heavy; I took a few cautionary steps back. Then I looked back at their haunting, decayed faces.

My mouth opened in a silent scream and I dropped to the floor beside them. They turned their heads to stare at me. Blood pooled around my knees, soaked into the thin material of my white nightgown. I watched, transfixed, while their decomposing arms moved up until decrepit, bony fingers pointed behind me. The expression in their dead stares widened in utter terror.

A hooded figure emerged from the shadows as I turned my head, the face obscured by the hood of the old, brown, monk-style robes he wore. He held a black candle, wax dripped down the sides and over his hands, red like molten blood.

I stood with infinite slowness and the figure stopped in front of me. Stretching my hand toward the head of the cloak, instinct told me I knew this stranger's identity. I threw the hood back and let out a blood-curdling scream at Daniel's half-lit face glaring back at me.

He dropped the candle. It ignited my nightgown. I screamed again and fell to the floor, using my hands to douse the flames with little effect. I held my blistered, melting palms in front of me in horror. Daniel kicked me onto my back, drew a knife from his robes, and plunged it toward my swollen belly.

Shooting bolt upright, I clutched my stomach. My breath came in short, sharp gasps and my hair stuck to my face from the sheen of perspiration blanketing my body. A headache gnawed at the base of my skull.

I looked over at the bedside clock—5:03am—the red numbers going in and out of focus, the room starting to spin around me.

Throwing the covers off me, I staggered out of bed and fumbled with the en-suite door. It crashed open against the wall as I hurtled toward the toilet. Bending over the bowl, I vomited the contents of my stomach into it. Spasms wracked my body while I gripped the toilet and wretched violently.

The last vestiges of my nightmare played over in my mind. My stomach continued to swirl.

Certain the nausea passed, I closed my eyes and leaned back against the wall. The icy sensation of the tiles soothed my feverish skin, and I took in shaky lungfuls of air before I stood. Approaching the basin, I turned the taps on and splashed cold water over my face and neck before gulping down a couple of handfuls.

On shaky legs, I made my way back to bed. The sheets were sodden with sweat and lay in a crumpled heap from my thrashing about. I climbed in and sat up against the headrest for a few moments, running the last few days over in my mind. I feared Daniel, I feared what he could do to me. But most of all, I feared for my unborn child.

∽∽∽

Candlelight illuminated the darkened room. Ivy sat alone, dead centre, eyes closed while she rocked back and forth.

"*Spiritus ducentia, protego me*," she chanted, volume increasing with each incantation.

Her words faltered with the fear she felt. Sweat beaded her forehead, her blonde hair plastered to her face and neck. She swiped it away with one hand while the other cradled her swollen belly. Tears fell down her pretty, pale face.

A faint noise startled her, followed by another and another. Her words faltered as she scanned the room, her gaze honing in on the closed door. *Still alone*.

Every breath came in short, sharp rasps while her body turned icy. Grabbing salt from a bowl beside her, she threw a handful over the candle in front, "*Protego me, protego me.*" Her voice grew urgent and she closed her eyes once again.

A lengthy creak stopped her midsentence and her breathing trembled with fright. Her heartbeat raced and, with sweaty palms, she balled and unballed her fists to rid herself of the prickling sensation.

She stared into the darkness. *They're here.*

The door burst open amid a huge gust of wind, extinguishing the majority of the candles. Her breath caught in her throat, and her eyes widened at the figure of the Priestess silhouetted before her—hand held up, palm outwards and clenched into a fist.

"*Tace!*" the Priestess shouted.

Ivy opened her mouth in a silent scream when the tall intruder stalked toward her. Her throat and lungs burned from the effort and the pressure built behind her ears with the exertion.

A light-haired witch followed the Priestess, striding to a shadowy corner of the room. The intruder spread her fingers and placed a palm on the wall now in front of her.

"*Egredietur spriritus, ego præcipio tibi, exi foras,*" she whispered.

Ivy turned to see a symbol burning through the paint. Smoke poured from it and the terrified girl watched a lazy trail drift in her direction.

Shaking her head in sheer panic, Ivy's eyes grew wide. She tried to get up only for the dark mist to race toward her. It knocked her down and curled around her wrists and ankles.

She thrashed wildly around on the floor, trying to scream. Her mouth flapped open, but no sound expelled. White hot pain twisted her insides as the flesh of her wrists seared through to the bone, the demonic fog relentless in its hold.

The Priestess loomed over her with a crazed grimace. Dim light glinted off the blade in her hand. The witch bore down and drove the weapon into her victim's chest. Fresh agony exploded in Ivy. Globules of deep, red blood spurted from the rent in her breast while she tried with desperation to break away.

Her life's essence ran warm and thick down her abdomen to pool beneath her. Hot tears coursed down her face. She wanted to beg for her life, for her baby's life with every pull of the blade toward her stomach. Writhing on the floor, she fought the veil of darkness creeping in.

Her body numbed after slow, torturous minutes, succumbing to the hellish pain. Her eyes closed and each breath became shallower than the last. Blood filled her throat, spilled from between her lips, while her struggles turned into odd, spasmodic twitches, before death claimed her in its slow, tormenting hold.

Through hazy vision she watched the Priestess remove the baby from her eviscerated womb—her baby. Sound filtered back, a death echo while she watched her baby move, heard him cry, then darkness swooped in on black wings.

Chapter 8

Amelia stood in the foyer of the Compound. She made small talk with Wendy while she waited for Nate. Evening approached and, after meeting with Sam and Chloe to discuss the second body, she sent them home and returned to the Compound.

"You'll get your key card soon, love, so no more waiting around." Wendy smiled at her.

The elevator doors pinged open and Nate strolled through. "We're ready for you." He winked at her and held out his hand.

With a scoff, Amelia walked straight past him and into the elevator. She heard Wendy giggle.

"You gonna leave me hanging?" He feigned hurt and placed his hand to his chest before following her in.

Amelia stared straight ahead with a smirk on her face.

The elevator took them up to the main living area, and from there Nate directed her to the Faction's labs.

Despite having been in the labs on several occasions, Amelia always marvelled at the sight—glass, chrome, light-wood. Ultramodern and full of high-tech equipment able to differentiate between normal human samples and those of the supernatural.

They stopped at a large table where two guys and a woman in lab coats, latex gloves and protective glasses, busied themselves examining some kind of residue in glass test tubes.

"Afternoon, Sebastian," Amelia smiled at him.

Sebastian stood tall with powerful, broad shoulders and brown hair shaved close to his head. Multiple piercings adorned his ears and one in his eyebrow, and tattoos emerged from the collar of his lab coat. Thick, brown eyebrows framed his smooth, shaved face and highlighted deep set, purple eyes.

He returned Amelia's smile, uttered something indiscernible to the other two lab geeks, then led Amelia and Nate toward the morgue.

They entered through stainless steel, double swing doors into a clinical space smelling of antiseptic and sandalwood freshener. Metal dissection tables stood in the centre of the room with more of the same stainless steel units, sinks, dissection apparatus and a large refrigeration unit Sebastian headed for.

He threw open adjoining doors of the unit and pulled out two sliding tables.

"What we looking at, big guy?" Nate glared at the plastic sheet-covered, lifeless forms in front of him.

Sebastian removed the material from the bodies. "Two vics. Female, Caucasian. Both early twenties and both with child, once upon a time. They were each in their final trimester, so both foetuses would have been fully formed.

"A sharp, uneven object was used to make either wound. The weapon used was a sacrificial knife, the blade carved from aged human bone and coated in polyurethane for preservation. There's trace residue on the skin. It cauterised as it cut.

"Both women died from massive trauma and exsanguination. In her initial prelim Amelia found the women were restrained supernaturally. My team is investigating the residue as we speak, but it looks likely."

"Any positive ID yet? Anything from the hairs collected at the scene?" Amelia queried. She stared between the unknown victims and wondered what family would be missing them.

"No ID yet, I'm afraid, but I do have something for you on those hair samples." He walked over to one of the steel cabinets and pulled out a plastic evidence bag. "Female, Caucasian with black hair. There isn't any blood on these samples, though, so this evidence is circumstantial at best. No follicular tags, either."

Amelia's shoulders slumped. "Anything on the claws?"

"Definitely owl claws, cut off with the same knife used to make the incisions in the stomachs given the jagged tool marks. The birds were dead when that happened."

"Thanks, Doc. Let's get outta here," Nate turned to Amelia.

"Where to?"

Before he could reply, his phone emitted a sharp ring. He halted in the doorway to fish it from his pocket. He answered, and continued into the corridor.

Amelia followed him through the doors.

"Tell me you're shitting me," he exclaimed, before he ended the call. He flicked his head in her direction, nostrils flared, jaw set. "We have another body. Victim's sister called it in. Blake and Deacon are at the scene already."

"Shit! Let's go."

Amelia called Chloe and Sam as they left the Compound; she reeled off the address and hung up.

The heavens opened and she ran for the gates, her foot tapping out an impatient beat while she waited for them to open.

"Ugh, I'm gonna smell like wet dog," Nate stated matter-of-factly, trudging to his van.

Amelia cast him a quick grin before she ran for her car.

Gunning the engine, she peeled off toward their new crime scene—Nate in tow.

∞∞∞

The September rain lashed down in torrents by the time Amelia and Nate arrived at the victim's farmhouse. Amelia's jeans stuck to her legs and the white t-shirt—she mentally kicked herself for wearing—got drenched to the point her black bra became visible through it.

Stationed outside the steel-gated entrance, Amelia spied one other car and a couple of bikes. *Great!* She would need to make a run for it up the dirt track to the main house.

Jumping from her vehicle, she raced up the driveway—Nate followed at a steadier pace.

Without a thought she barged straight through the front door—eager to get out of the torrential rainstorm outside—and bounced straight off Blake's rock-hard torso.

"Well, well. I see you've made the effort for me," he smirked, brows raised while he stared wide-eyed and without shame at her chest.

Amelia rolled her eyes at him, "You're nothing if not predictable." She crossed her arms over her chest, but it didn't make the slightest bit of difference.

"Oh, believe me when I tell you, I am so much more than that." He flashed that smile again, and gave her a devilish wink.

Amelia's cheeks flushed, despite an attempt to suppress her smile. *What the hell? You're a thirty-two year old woman; you don't get embarrassed by a man!* she thought. *Yes, but look at him!?* And she did—the blond-haired, beautiful, toned definition of sex stood staring at her.

She shouldered her way past Blake, making sure to catch him.

The large kitchen boasted several off-white, lattice-windowed cupboards with light oak work surfaces, an envious Aga stove and a large island bar in the middle with a pots and pans wire rack above it—all very Country Living.

Deacon stood to one side of the bar talking to Chloe and Sam, who, judging by their soaking wet clothes and hair, came fresh from outside themselves.

"Damn, I need to get my kit out of my car." Amelia padded the pockets of her jacket in search of her keys.

"I'll go for you," Blake leant in close and whispered the words in her ear, his hand on the small of her back.

Curling his hand around her waist in a slow, sweet motion, Amelia's breath hitched. With his lips still close to her neck, her heart rate quickened and the warmth of his breath on her skin caused a shiver to shoot down her spine.

Snaking his hand further around, Blake delved into the pocket of Amelia's blazer. He pulled out her car keys and bolted out the door in a blur.

Amelia released her breath, only to suck it in again when Blake reappeared in front of her. He placed her kit on the bar, and sauntered over to her, handing her the car keys. An electrifying ripple shot through her skin when his hand brushed hers. She fought the desire to close her eyes and imagine--

"Scene's upstairs," Deacon's voice knocked Amelia out of her erotic trance.

With a quick mental shake of her senses, she motioned for him to lead the way. Blake remained in the kitchen while Deacon took everyone else upstairs.

Positioned on the landing Amelia could see four doors, three already open, their contents signifying two bedrooms and a bathroom. The other remained closed.

Amelia pressed forward and, putting on latex gloves, pushed the doors inwards with due caution.

The smell hit her first—the same stench of fear and death intermingled, but also a mixture of urine and blood; the copper scent the stronger of the two. Amelia dealt with blood on a regular basis, but in such a confined space the stench always overpowered her.

Gloom permeated the area thanks to the drawn blackout curtains, but Amelia made out the outline of the victim lying in the centre of the dark wood floor. She felt her way along the wall for a switch, and flipped it when she found it. Light bathed the room in a dull glow giving Amelia view of the bloody, half-naked body outstretched amid a disturbed circle of salt. Small splashes of blood sprayed the walls, floor and furniture.

An altar stood at the far end of the room; dark wood with one shelf attached at the top. It housed a large book, or tome, leather bound with gold clasps; the paper looked like dated parchment. Amelia could see dark writing, but couldn't make any of it out from where she stood. Numerous candles in various states of use were positioned on shelves and around the floor; some black, some red, some white.

On one of the deep red-painted walls Amelia noted the familiar symbol of Lilith with the same smoke emanating from whatever once lay beneath. A large wardrobe dominated most of the left hand wall with various other items around the room; bones, charms, trinket bags. However, the centre of the room drew Amelia's immediate attention.

Moving closer, Amelia detected the same gaping hole in the victim's chest; it ran from her chest, the length of her stomach and down to her groin. The face remained untouched, save for the splatters of blood, and Amelia detected the same burn marks around her wrists and ankles. Leaning in, she noticed something wedged in the victim's throat.

"Careful, she might try to tongue you."

Amelia turned to see Sam in the doorway, grinning like a buffoon.

"Even a dead victim with their stomach slashed open would be a step up from the states that've had their tongues down your throat." Amelia cast him a smug smile before making her way out the bedroom.

Sam glared at her. His mouth flapped open, but promptly closed with no hint of a comeback.

"Check out the other rooms," she instructed.

Nate waltzed past her into the murder scene to conduct his collection of evidence, after she highlighted the object in their victim's throat.

Chloe followed to give a hand with photographs, though, faltered when she caught sight of the mangled body.

Amelia turned to Deacon, "Someone called this in, do we have an ID?"

"Ivy Swanson," Deacon responded.

"Her sister called you guys?"

Deacon nodded. "Yes."

"Where is she now?"

The vampire shrugged, "We don't know. No one was here when we arrived."

"Are we sure it was the sister?" Amelia queried.

"Yeah, she said as much on the phone and I don't see why the witches would wanna call in their own murder scene."

Amelia nodded and stared into the distance in thought. "I agree. We need to track her down; she might've seen something that can help."

"I'll call for a search," Deacon offered. He pulled his mobile from his back pocket.

Sam appeared back on the landing. "What about the father?"

Amelia pondered over it for a moment before she popped her head in the altar room. "Roberts, see if you can find any pictures of the vic's sister, as well as a name, and any pictures of a boyfriend or husband. Gather whatever evidence you find downstairs, then go check around the perimeter, see if you can find anything that might indicate where this missing sister went to. Take Blake and Chapman with you."

"Yes, ma'am," Chloe replied, making her way downstairs.

Amelia walked back into the room where Nate busied himself with the evidence. "Same kinda stuff?"

"Looks that way. Owl's claw in throat, burnt residue on wrists and ankles, and the same wounds. There is one difference, though."

Crouching beside him, she asked, "Why's that?"

"You said before that the witches were using demons to restrain these women."

"That's right."

Nate tilted his head in Amelia's direction, "Then either Ivy managed to put up a bit of a fight before she was held down, or the killer slipped up. There's trace evidence underneath her fingernails."

Chapter 9

I spent my day wandering the Compound. I chatted with Wendy and got a general feel for the place I would call home for the next few days—at least, I hoped it wouldn't be any longer than that.

Some of my reservations and fears dwindled the moment Deacon's gaze captured mine. When he touched me, fireworks erupted through my body and I felt safe, protected. I knew my daughter and I would be secure here, but for how long? What would happen when the time came to leave? Would the police have found Daniel by then? And what of Deacon?

My soul yearned for his closeness in a way that both scared and excited me. Inside me grew another man's child—a man I never really knew, a man I feared. A man hell bent on kidnapping my daughter.

Deacon made me forget. In such a short space of time, I found myself pining for a man I feared could never be mine. To expect him to raise another man's baby... what did all this make me?

It wouldn't do me well to dwell on a situation I couldn't change.

But I couldn't help it.

To ease my tension somewhat, I spent a good amount of time in the Compound's library reading baby book after baby book after cheesy, raunchy romance novel. I even spent some time trawling the internet, adding numerous pink toys and clothes to several online shopping baskets. But then I remembered I had no home for which to have them delivered, and next to no money to purchase them.

I spoke to Alice before she started her shift at the pub. Not having spoken to her for a day or so, I had hoped she could share with me some juicy piece of gossip, anything I could ponder over needlessly to distract from my predicament... and the nightmares that plagued me.

Alice's parents took on a new member of staff at the pub for the busy autumn nights—not all that juicy, but still. She did grab my attention when she told me she'd driven by my house a few times. Still no sign of Daniel, though. The mention of his name brought back the vivid image of his shadowed glare before he... drove... that knife. The recollection made my heart race and my skin break out in goose bumps.

Now, sat in the kitchen at the Compound, I put my fears aside once again. He couldn't get me here. The police would catch him and I would be able to return home. Me and my daughter wouldn't have to worry about him ever again.

My stomach rumbled.

Lucky for me, after a quick rummage, I found the fridges stocked with edible food. I put together a basic chicken salad, and, sick of the confines of my room, sat at the island bar to eat it.

The door to my right opened and a tall, slim woman with long, dark blonde hair walked in.

She hesitated at the door, "Oh, sorry, I didn't realise anybody was in here."

"That's OK," I smiled, "just grabbing some lunch before I starved."

She looked at my empty plate, then my swollen tummy. *Nope, no blood. I'm not a vampire.*

"Do you live here?" she asked me with a crumpled expression while she grabbed a bottle of water from the fridge.

Shaking my head, I responded, "No, I'm just staying here temporarily."

The lady sat down next to me and eyed me with a long glance. "I'm Amelia."

"Elora." Amelia shook my offered hand.

"Elora? B's daughter?"

I laughed, not surprised everyone knew my dad. "Yeah, do you work with him?"

"No, I'm a DCI with the Lancashire Constabulary. I help out with certain case types. How come you're here? I don't recall B ever telling me you had supernatural abilities." She smiled at, a chuckle filtering past her lips. "Sorry, bad joke."

I curled into myself and looked away from her stare. "I don't... I... um... ."

"It's OK; you don't have to tell me if you don't want to."

What do I have to lose—this woman is a police officer? "I'm in hiding, I suppose. My ex-boyfriend assaulted me and threatened to take my baby from me." My hands slipped to my belly.

Amelia's breath hitched as her sympathetic gaze eyed me cradling my bump. "I'm sorry to hear that. Did you report him?"

"Yes." I nodded, eyes still averted. "Only... he's gone missing."

"What's his name?"

"Dan--"

Before we could talk any more, Blake barged into the kitchen with all the finesse of a British Bulldog.

"Sorry to break up the party girlies, but I need to steal Amelia away."

Amelia turned to smile at me. "It was nice meeting you. Maybe we can carry on our chat another time?"

"Sure, I'd like that." And I really would—I liked her. I could almost feel her soul speaking to me—kind, protective, yet fearless.

It worried me how I knew that.

∞ ∞ ∞

Amelia and Blake joined Lucas and Deacon in the conference room.

"Go ahead boss; tell her what you just told us." Blake directed his statement at Lucas.

"Take a seat, Amelia."

She positioned herself in a chair in front of Lucas. Blake sat down beside her.

"We've had an anonymous phone call from a woman who claims to be a witch," Lucas continued, sliding a copy of the phone transcript over to Amelia.

Amelia's interest piqued. "Is she good or bad?"

"Good. She claims to be a member of the coven of the three murder victims."

Amelia's eyes widened. "They were all from the same coven?"

"That's right," Lucas rifled through the notes in front of him. "The scripture from the book at the Swanson place was mainly spells and incantations. It did acknowledge three witches, though; Morgan, Gill and Belle."

Taking in a breath, Amelia curbed her premature excitement. "No surnames? We need to track these women down; perhaps they know something; maybe they're involved somehow."

"With no surnames it'll be difficult to narrow down, but I'll have someone work on it."

"How does the caller know the others have been murdered? We've not released any details yet."

"That's the kicker. She reckons she saw it before it happened."

Amelia raised her brow, "Psychic? Did she say who it was? And why now?"

"She didn't stay on the line long enough for us to ask too many questions, but she fears she could be next."

Amelia hesitated, studying Lucas' words. "She's pregnant?"

"Yes. Almost to term."

"She can't be the only pregnant witch in the County. Why else would she think she's being targeted?"

"She says she knows how the victims were chosen."

Amelia considered Lucas's rigid facial expression. "She hasn't told us, though."

Lucas shook his head.

"Bollocks. Do we have an address?" she concluded.

"Someone's working on that now."

On cue a short, young woman with waist-long, box-dyed red hair and violet eyes walked into the room. She held a sheet of paper. Dressed in a small, denim skirt, a tight, skull-motif tank top and spiked, platform calf-boots, she looked like a gothic harlot.

"Amelia, this is Ember Belrose, she's from another Faction, but she's fantastic with a computer. She's offered to help track down anything we can, to get ID's on our girls."

Ember ignored his words, instead she shifted straight over to Deacon and stared at him like a schoolgirl with a crush. She smiled sickly-sweet, flashing her fangs, and placed the paper down, brushing her showcased breasts against his arm—the reason behind her choice of revealing apparel now clear to Amelia.

"Here's the address you wanted. It's under the name Belinda Larkin." She spoke only to Deacon.

He didn't glance at her and Amelia caught the uncomfortable look marring his features—proof he didn't appreciate the smitten vampire. He still didn't make eye contact when he spoke to her.

"Thanks, Ember. That'll be all for now." He sighed, heavy with agitation.

Ember didn't notice—or care—Deacon's statement meant 'sod off, you're no longer needed'. She gazed at him with a dreamy look in her large, dilated eyes. Amelia couldn't recall a time a vampire acted so... credulous.

"If you need me to do anything else, just ask." She sauntered out of the room, glancing back at Deacon to see if he noticed her. He didn't turn his head.

Amused, Amelia grabbed the piece of paper and studied the address. "This must be our Belle. I know where this is, I can go tonight."

"Don't you think it's a bit late, now?" Blake rested his chin on his hand and stared at her.

"The later we leave it the more likely she is to skip out on us. There's a reason she didn't give her name or location."

"It's dark enough now. The two of you go together," Lucas instructed them, "Deacon and I have work to do here."

Amelia's heart leapt into her mouth at the prospect of being alone again with Blake. Her breathing rate picked up and she felt a little nervous, *or is it excitement?* Perhaps both.

"Let's get this show on the road, then, sweetheart."

He winked at her and her resolve waned.

∞∞∞

It took twenty minutes to get to the address Ember gave them. Pulling up across the road, Amelia and Blake observed the building. There were no lights on, in or around the property.

"What now?" Blake's gaze remained fixed out the window, toward the house.

Amelia caught his stare, shook her head and smirked. "It's a bloody good job I'm here. You'd stand no chance being a copper."

"What do you mean?" Blake's eyes widened in disbelief.

"It might look as though no one is home, Ace, but we still gotta check it out. Looks can be deceiving."

Blake curled his lips up at her. "Can't they just?" He waggled his brows.

Amelia reddened and turned her head away before they climbed out of the car.

They made their way up the paved drive and knocked on the front door. To Amelia's shock and dismay the door swung open on its own.

"Crap." Removing her police issue baton from her belt, she glanced at Blake and cocked her eyebrow.

She stepped over the threshold with caution, and into the hallway of Belinda's home. The place looked like a tornado ran amok—furniture lay strewn about, broken picture frames hung in disarray on the walls and broken ornaments and glass littered the floor.

Amelia didn't switch any lights on. She motioned for Blake to go ahead of her and check what looked to be a kitchen while she examined the front room.

Blake held back from using his natural speed—not sure who they were dealing with or what power they might yield, he wanted to be vigilant. Not only that, but he took Amelia's welfare into consideration, he'd be damned if she came to harm because of his thoughtlessness.

He made his way into a large kitchen in a very similar state to the hallway—the place not only ripped apart, but blown to smithereens. Scorch marks lined intermittent areas of the wall, floor and ceiling as though someone lost control of a flamethrower... or magic, out of sheer, frustrated anger.

Nothing else jumped out at him, so he made his way toward the stairs he saw in the hallway when they entered. He passed the living room and watched, in muted fascination, when Amelia bent down to examine the extent of some of the chaos in the room. Her dark jeans stretched across her pert arse and he stifled a growl. *Damn, she is hot.*

Tearing his gaze away, he walked up the stairs to the landing. Three doors hung off their hinges and each room showed similar signs of destruction to downstairs. One door remained ajar, but Blake doubted he would find anything less than comparable damage inside.

His hand stilled over the doorknob—he could smell burning sulphur in the air and something else. Like the smell you got during a rain storm moments before lightning struck.

A force, hot and powerful, exploded from the room. It powered into his chest. Both he and the remainder of the door flew over the handrail and crashed down the stairs. He landed, dazed at the bottom with a heavy thud before the screech of tires tore off and a blurred shape shot by him with unimaginable speed.

Amelia's scream preceded an almighty crash. His fangs descended and he shot to his feet, drawn between going after the unknown, the car or making sure Amelia hadn't come to harm. He didn't need to think about it— he shook himself off and raced into the living room, but he couldn't see the DCI anywhere.

A strong gust blew debris around the room and Blake looked toward the window to see a jagged, gaping hole, the dark curtains flapping violently in the wind. Without a second thought, he pounced onto the sofa in front, straight onto the windowsill and out into the front garden.

Amelia lay about five feet in front of him, face down and splayed out. Blake could see pieces of glass in her hair and on her back. He flew to her side, but didn't dare to move her for fear of making matters worse.

"Amelia, can you hear me?" His hand hovered over her stirring form. "Don't move, I'll call for help."

Muffled by the grass beneath her, she mumbled, "I'm fine," while she struggled to get up.

The effort proved to be too much and she only succeeded in turning over, landing awkwardly on her back, the wind knocked out of her.

"What the hell happened?" She palmed a bloody patch on her head.

"I have no idea. Whoever got here before us was still inside."

Blake looked down at her body and noticed a nasty gash near her shoulder where glass sliced through shirt and flesh. Other than that, and the cut on her head, she seemed otherwise unharmed—from the outside at least.

"Why didn't you go after them?"

Blake's fangs withdrew, knocked back by her question, or perhaps the truth behind his answer made him hesitate? "Because I didn't know what happened do you."

"Since when did you care, big guy?" She half-smiled.

Blake grinned back at her. "Come on. I think it's safe to say no one is home. We need to get you seen to. Can you move?"

"Yeah, I think so. My ankle feels a bit dodgy, and then there is the matter of my bruised pride."

Blake laughed at her, a genuine, hearty sound derived from his relief.

∞ ∞ ∞

A faint knock sounded against my door. Placing my book down I pulled myself off the bed and moved to open it.

I held back a gasp at the sight of Deacon's beautiful, sparkling eyes.

My tongue went cotton wool dry when I tried to speak. Words fired around my brain, but not one made it out of my lips to form a coherent sentence.

He looked every bit the beefy hunk, even in grey track bottoms and a tight, white vest. His sculpted arms and shoulders glistened under the dim light with post workout perspiration.

I drank him in with lust-fuelled hunger before I snapped my eyes back to his.

"H-hi," I stammered through my constricted throat. *Must remember to swallow, must remember to swallow… must remember to breathe!*

"Hi, yourself." His smile took my breath away.

I stepped aside, "You wanna come in?"

He glided into the room, closing the door behind him. "I'm sorry I haven't been around much, I--"

"It's OK," I smiled at him with reassurance, "you have a job to do."

He avoided my gaze, but he looked disconsolate with sad, wide eyes, his breathing heavy. Work perhaps? *Or is it me?*

"No, it isn't you." His words were hasty, and he turned back to me with desperate longing in his dovelike stare.

Did he just read my mind?

Hands on my hips, I looked into his eyes. *Crap!* If he could read my mind, what... *Oh my God*... my inner most thoughts about him, what I felt, what I wanted him to do to me.

He took hold of my shoulders in his large hands and pressed his body close. With one long, hungry look he crushed his lips against mine in a swift, urgent movement.

I melted against him and moaned into his mouth as his agile tongue found mine.

He broke away. "I'm sorry, I didn't...," he stammered.

I touched my tingling lips with a light caress. My heart melted when I looked back at the sadness in Deacon's eyes.

"Deacon, are you OK? You don't have to apologise for what just happened." Then I whispered, "I wanted it."

So many mixed emotions ran through my mind. Guilt ate away at me. His kiss left my legs weak and my stomach in knots, but being pregnant with another man's child… should I want this?

Every fibre of my being yearned for this man in front of me. A burning fire raged through me with one look from him. One touch batted my senses around my brain like a thousand bullets ricocheting off metal walls.

But it felt unbelievably right—strong and very real.

Despite the incredibly short time in which we'd known each other, every moment away from him felt like one half of my soul was missing. An emptiness clawed through my body. I couldn't fight it, even if I wanted to.

But Daniel remained in the back of my mind. His threat. Those he implied were after me. With my head in such a state; scared for the life of my child and me… it wouldn't be fair to drag someone into this. *This is my emotional burden to bear.*

Moving in closer, he whispered, "I'll protect you."

A multitude of sparks fired off in my brain. His face so close, I could feel his hot breath trickle down my neck. Why would this man—this gorgeous, beautiful, strong man—want to protect me. When I placed a hand over my belly, he placed his straight over.

"I'll protect your child as well."

Deacon pressed the pad of his thumb to the single tear sliding down my cheek. I closed my eyes at the tenderness of his caress—familiar tantalizing currents roused my body.

My heart pounded and endless sounds filtered through the open window—water rippled, owls hooted, animals scurried, trees rustled in the thrashing wind.

Deacon's laboured breathing overpowered my senses, his hand still touched my face. I opened my eyes and the noises subsided, but the sensations lingered. I stared at his luscious, pink lips—parted to let out his unsteady breathing.

Shifting my gaze, I looked into his intense stare. "Deac--"

He brushed his lips against mine—gentle, delicate, not desperate and rushed like before. My body went numb and he pulled me closer, holding me with his free hand. His tongue explored my lips, darted around my mouth and clashed with my tongue in the most sensual, erotic kiss. My stomach flipped and I throbbed in places long forgotten, experiencing urges not felt for years.

Placing a hand on his hip, I used my other to grab at his shoulders, neck, face, before I brought them both up to run through his silky hair.

I weakened at the growl rumbling in his chest. Disembodied, all I sensed, all I could focus on were his lips on mine—I melted further into his hold when he snaked one hand from my face to the back of my neck—deepening the kiss.

His impressive erection strained against my thigh and my mind emptied of all other thoughts, except for this man's rock hard body pressed against me. How his powerful hands held me close and how his lips brushed against mine, so soft and moist.

He broke away all too soon, and I moaned my disappointment.

Placing his hand back against my cheek, he whispered, "I'll protect you both, I swear on my life."

And I didn't doubt his promise for a second.

Chapter 10

I ran, hard and fast, my breathing fitful, lungs ready to burst at any moment, but still I ran. My bare feet bled and my legs felt injected with lead, but I didn't stop, not until I reached the clearing. Sweat bathed my body, while I ached and struggled for breath.

Rocks were positioned in a makeshift circular pattern on the uneven, muddy ground. White rags caught in the surrounding trees flapped like wild spectres in the strong, blustering wind. Rain battered my face, ran into my eyes and round the contours of my mouth.

Stepping into the centre of the circle, the wind stopped whirling my hair around my face, the rain ceased to pound at my body, yet it still went on outside whatever bubble I walked into.

After a few deep breaths, I ran my hands over my face to wipe away the water. I heard a muffled cry and I stopped, cocked my head to the side and tried to make out where it came from.

I noticed a shallow ditch nearby. I advanced toward it with caution. I sensed something bad—a feeling of dread rushed up my body, making me shiver. The cry came again. Is that a baby? I couldn't leave a baby out here in this cold.

Approaching the hole, branches cracked under my weight and mud squelched in between my toes. I knelt down beside it. A bundle covered in dark-stained rags lay within. My outstretched hand stilled; I swore I heard someone whisper my name—a female someone. A voice I didn't recognise. But then, would I recognise something so inaudible?

It didn't come again, so I reached into the pit and dragged the tattered rags out.

A baby lay beneath, eyes closed while she cried. I picked her up and wrapped her in the cloth used to shelter her from the elements. She looked so tiny and innocent, who would leave her outside in this?

Cooing her, I tickled under her chin, she tried to smile and grab for my finger. I heard my whispered name again and gasped. Swiping my head from left to right, I looked around the dense wooded area. I couldn't see or sense anything, nothing at all.

Dropping my gaze back to the child, I resolved to take her out of here, but when I looked at her, her eyes rolled back to reveal milky white orbs and her mouth opened in a silent scream. I shrieked and the baby wriggled from my grasp, but just before the girl hit the ground, she turned into an owl and flew off into the night, screeching an ear piercing sound.

For long moments I stood rooted.

My surroundings melted together into an all-consuming blackness. My body dropped and I plummeted into depths unknown. My arms and legs flailed around as I tried to gain a control that didn't exist.

I landed on my back on a mound of pillows and lay there for a few seconds while I gained my composure. 'Elora', I heard it again, more distinct this time; female for sure.

Sitting bolt upright, in an underground chamber of sorts, I eyed the monastery-type surrounding. I spied monk-looking characters ambling about the place. Their brown robes looked familiar.

They hovered near an altar and I dragged myself up from the ground to take a closer look. Something lay on the altar—something small and very fidgety.

Holy Hell, another baby! A dreaded sensation swirled in the pit of my stomach, and I tried to cry out. No sound erupted from between my lips. In fact, no sound came *from anywhere. I looked at the screaming baby, but I couldn't hear its cries.*

I grabbed at my stomach... shit! Oh, God no! My bump, where is my baby? Realisation smacked me straight in the face. I looked back at the altar, wide-eyed with sickening fear, my mouth open in shock and disbelief.

I didn't need to find my voice when I saw one of the robed figures draw a knife from their belt and aim it at my child! I lurched forwards, but one of the cloaked bodies turned towards me, threw out their hand and emitted a burning ball of white hot fire. It hurtled straight for me and hit me square in the chest.

I woke screaming in agony, my entire body bathed in sweat, my chest tight and heavy. Clutching at it, I writhed around the bed.

"Ellie, what's wrong?" Deacon's terrified voice panicked me.

I couldn't answer him, though—I only wanted to scream until the pain went away. I clutched my chest tighter and Deacon put one hand to it while the other went to my forehead. His cold skin soothed the raging inferno gushing over my body.

"Jesus, you're on fire, and your heart is going a million miles per hour."

With squinted eyes, I watched Deacon drag the covers off of me. He stared at me with a look of sheer horror on his face. His nose twitched and flared and his hand went up to cover his mouth.

"Holy fucking Christ, Elora, you're bleeding!" he exclaimed, before grabbing his phone.

∞∞∞

Amelia hated hospitals; she associated them with sadness and death. The Compound's medical institution, however, didn't creep her out quite so much. The usual antiseptic aroma didn't linger, and the decor—ultra sleek and hi tech—definitely did not belong in your run of the mill hospital.

Her own spacious room's three walls were frosted glass, but the back—housing the bed—soft oak panelling. The adornments were all modern and very tasteful, high-gloss, white units—one of which held a brand new LCD TV.

She sat beside Blake on the large bed. The pain from her ankle subsided, but her head comprised a couple of butterfly stitches, and a gauze pad dressed the gash below her collarbone.

She stared at the floor, her mind replaying the night's events.

"Did you see anything?" Blake broke the silence.

Her head snapped up and she squinted her eyes against the throb of her injuries. "Yeah... my life flashing before my eyes as I careened through a glass window! What the hell did you think I saw?" She glared into his eyes.

Blake balked at the vehemence in her voice and opened his mouth only to close it again seconds later.

Amelia put her head in her hands, careful to avoid her wound. "I'm sorry, I didn't mean to snap," she sighed, running her hands over her hair before looking into his eyes. "I'm just frustrated that they were there... right in our grasp, and I let them slip by."

"It wasn't your fault, Amelia. Even I couldn't get a hold of whoever, or whatever, was there. I should've known; should've helped you."

Amelia slid off the bed and paced the ward with a slight limp. She swung back around to face Blake. "You couldn't have done anything. Whatever hurtled me through the window wasn't human."

"I know. But that means… ."

"The witches have someone working for them, and we need to find out who or what it is."

Amelia jumped when the Faction's Doctor, Jacob sped past the open door with a gurney, several staff members at his heels. Moments later he ran back with someone on the table, screaming in agony. Deacon rushed close behind, his face contorted in anxious panic.

"What the hell… ." Blake's statement hung in the air while he and Amelia made their way out of the room to follow the procession.

Amelia struggled to keep up while Blake, Deacon and Jacob used their speed to get to their destination. She slowed down when she saw Jacob enter the operating theatre. He instructed Deacon and Blake to remain behind.

She caught the last part of Jacob's instruction.

"... nothing you can do right now, Deak. Sit down. She's in good hands."

Deacon growled, his fangs descended. He smashed his fist through the wall next to the doors Jacob disappeared through. Plaster and dust erupted from the gaping hole and the vibrations shook the surface, reverberating around the room.

"What's happened, bro?" Blake's hand faltered over Deacon's heaving shoulders.

Amelia knew Deacon held a good hundred years or more on Blake—their strength grew with age—and it would be wise for Blake to refrain from causing Deacon to lash out without a thought.

"Was that Elora?" Amelia panted.

"Yes," Deacon answered through clenched teeth, hand still splayed beside the hole he created.

"Is she... OK?" Blake hesitated.

"I don't know... the baby... ." He spun around, fangs rescinding while he ran a hand through his dark hair and grabbed the side of his head with both palms, his frantic, wide eyes darting from person to person.

Blake and Amelia stared at a despairing Deacon while he paced the corridor. He stared at the floor, fists now balled at his sides.

A few minutes passed before all three were startled when another set of doors burst open and Bernie rushed through.

"Where is she? Is she OK? What's happening to her?" He almost collided with Deacon in his haste to reach his daughter.

"I-I don't know," the warrior stammered. "I went to see her, she asked me to stay while she slept. She started thrashing about and woke up clutching her chest. I could smell blood, a lot of it, and when I drew back the covers the sheets were soaked in it."

Amelia and Bernie gasped, but Bernie recovered first.

"Is the baby...?" His stricken face paled.

Deacon hung his head, "I don't know."

"She's lucky you were there." Blake risked putting his hand on Deacon's shoulder. "Jacob's the best at what he does. He'll make sure she's OK."

The minutes stretched into an eternity before Jacob walked through the operating theatre's doors. Amelia wished her frame of mind could appreciate his masculine good looks.

He wore a dishevelled lab coat over his green combat trousers and grey tank top.

He removed the coat and stepped further into the corridor and Amelia could almost admire the sculpted curves of his well-toned body. Tattoos ran up both arms, but stopped before his neck line.

"Please tell me she's OK, Jacob," Bernie pleaded with him, but stopped short of grabbing Jacob by the arms.

The doctor placed a gentle hand on Bernie's shoulder and soothed, "She's gonna be fine, B. She's lost a bit of blood, but we've set her up with a transfusion."

Bernie ran a hand over his pallid face, then through unkempt hair. "My grandchild... ?"

"... Is just fine. Elora's body reacted to a stressful situation. She had a nightmare, but there's no cause for alarm anymore."

"What about her chest? She was grabbing at her chest," Deacon implored, his eyes enlarged.

"A simple panic attack. Her nightmare spooked her a little more than it should have and she started to panic."

Everyone in the room let out a sigh of relief and Jacob offered reassuring smiles.

Bernie took a step closer to the doctor. "Can I see her?"

"She's sedated at the moment. I want her to get some rest before she deals with any visitors. I need to be sure she won't have another reaction."

"But she's my daughter!" Bernie exclaimed, his brow wrinkling above wide eyes.

"And she's my patient, B." Jacob put a hand on Bernie's shoulder and gave him a gentle shake. "Let me do my job and make sure she's one hundred percent."

Bernie hung his head and nodded his understanding before Jacob walked back through the doors. Bernie turned to Deacon.

"You were there? What happened?"

"When I went to see her, she asked me to stay with her. She wanted to feel protected, she told me. I sat beside her while she slept. As I was about to leave she started to thrash about, I called her. She woke up screaming."

"She seems to be in good hands now, though, and safe," Amelia added, trying to inject some assurances into the guys.

Deacon didn't notice her presence until now—he eyed her injuries. "What happened to you?"

"She had an argument with a window. Believe it or not the window came off worse." Blake flashed a smile at Amelia.

The DCI looked at him, unimpressed, and rolled her eyes before she focused her attention back on Deacon. "We went to check out that address, but something beat us to it."

"Something?" Deacon's brow dipped and he cocked his head.

Blake nodded. "Whatever it was, it wasn't human. It was fast. Faster than me, and powerful."

"Had it gotten to Belinda?"

"Not that we could see. I think whatever it was realised that she wasn't home, just as we came on the scene. It blasted something at me that knocked me for six before throwing Amelia out of a window."

"Jesus," Bernie breathed.

"You didn't see it then?" Deacon pursed his lips.

Amelia shook her head, "No, it was way too fast and a complete blur. I did get a partial plate number on the car that was parked near the house, though."

"You did?" Blake and Deacon asked in unison, Blake with notes of surprise in his voice and Deacon with angst.

Amelia nodded, she forgot to mention it earlier—she blamed the blow to the head. "I've already given the details to Ember. She's looking into it for us."

"How did you manage that? You were inhaling dirt when I found you," Blake raised a brow in question.

"Noted it before we went inside. It was parked on double yellows with no indicator... I am good at what I do ya know."

Blake's lips twisted into a smile.

"Good thing one of you is," Deacon glared at Blake with a look of slight humour dancing about his features.

He visibly relaxed after Jacob's visit; his shoulders lost some of their tension and he no longer clenched and unclenched his fists.

With the moment of silence that followed, he looked toward the theatre doors. His chest puffed out as he inhaled a deep breath, and his jaw went rigid.

Elora meant something to him; that much became clear. His stiff posture, while he glared at the doors, told Amelia—as she watched his laboured breathing—he wanted Elora safe, well and protected.

∞∞∞

Amelia's injuries didn't deter her from the job at hand. Reluctant to leave, lest more information filter through, she joined Blake on the sofa in the living area. However, exhaustion began to creep up and settle in her bones.

Her body relaxed, and random images filtered into her subconscious as she dozed.

Solid arms lifted her off the sofa, and her eyes flickered open to see Blake's handsome face smiling down at her.

"You were starting to drool on my shoulder," he whispered to her through his wide grin.

She hummed an incomprehensible sound and snuggled her head into his rock hard body.

A chuckle rumbled through Blake's chest and Amelia's eyes sprang open. She wriggled out of Blake's grip and he laughed harder. He grappled with her to place her on her feet in order stop her falling arse first onto the floor.

Amelia brushed herself off and cleared her throat a few times, avoiding Blake's gaze. She smoothed her hair back and hissed when her fingers caught the stitches on her head.

"Sorry. I--"

"You don't have to apologise, Amelia."

Her name sounded so rich and warm rolling off his tongue. Her face heated. She shook herself off, straightened her back and puffed out her chest. Big mistake. Blake's eyes zoomed right in on her breasts.

She narrowed her eyes at him and pouted her lips. Crossing her arms over her chest, she continued walking. With a quick glance back in his direction, she caught sight of that damn sexy grin of his.

"Don't be shy, babe." He drawled.

Babe? What a nerve this guy's got. She tried to convince herself of his rudeness, pet names usually reserved for intimate couples. She *tried* telling herself that, when in reality the moment the word left his lips, her stomach vaulted straight into her throat.

No, no, no. I am a professional bloody police officer, working a case with these guys—affectionate terms of endearment were not appropriate... not until they completed their assignment at least. She needed to get her shit together.

"I'm going to bed, I'll--"

"That's exactly where I was taking you." Blake threw her a sly smile.

Damn it! Screw him and his sexual innuendos and his drop dead gorgeous face and his sexy-ass smile. Screw him all to hell. He's toying with me, teasing me, just like she did to him.

Despite the pain in her head and shoulder, she let herself enjoy every damn minute of his flirty behaviour. Even with shrouded judgment from the night's events, she couldn't sustain her imaginary annoyance. The back and forth between them stirred excitement deep within her, stoked the embers of a fire lit the moment she saw him. *And two can play this game.*

"I've told you before; I can do things for myself."

"You have, but you don't have to… just so you know."

God damn it, he could not win. Her face burned, *no way am I having this*, absolutely no way would he be allowed to think he got under her skin.

"Duly noted, Ace. But I know how I like things done." She winked at his smirking face.

Yes! One point, Amelia. Up yours, vampire boy! she thought.

"There's nothing wrong with change," he countered. With a quick twitch of his head, he winked back.

Anticipating such a response—timed to perfection—she opened the door to her room and stepped inside.

"That's yet to be proved to me."

She cast him her best sultry smile and closed the door on him. Her smile widened when she heard his low growl from the other side.

*

Damn it! Damn that woman and the things she could do to him. She made his body react with purely feral urges. His blood boiled and his whole body screamed to be pressed tight against hers—*and she knows it.*

The more she played this game the more determined Blake became to claim her for himself—every part of her. He wanted to make her body quake for his touch just by breathing her name, to feel every inch of her pulsate for the need to be taken in every way he could possibly dream of—and he dreamed of a few.

He wanted to watch the pure ecstasy spread across her face when he did things to her body she probably only read about. The mere thought of her hot, naked, writhing form beneath him caused an erection to strain painfully against his jeans.

He remained outside her room, breathing in her scent—he could sense her on the other side, leaning against the door. He could feel her heart beat though it and imagined hearing her take deep, drawn-out breaths because she, hopefully, harboured similar thoughts about him.

Chapter 11

A serene calmness swept over me. My eyes were closed, but I could hear birds singing; melodic alongside the high pitched chirps of grasshoppers—nature's own orchestra. The sun beat down on my face, and I smiled in the warmth, my whole body tingling. A slight breeze tickled my flesh and goose bumps puckered my skin, but I still felt delightfully flushed under the sun's beating rays.

My eyes fluttered open and I gazed into the clear blue sky—not a cloud in sight, beautiful. I didn't remember feeling this peaceful in a long time. I didn't want it to end.

I turned my head to the side and noticed I lay in a field upon lush, green grass. With no-one else in sight, I smiled at the tranquil solitude. Stretching out, I fisted the grass at my sides.

A gentle echo travelled along the breeze—a soft whisper, and I raised myself to my elbows to properly investigate my surroundings. Nothing but vast stretches of open countryside, the odd tree imposed upon the otherwise sweeping expanse. But I could see nothing that might have caused the noise I heard.

About to chalk it up to my imagination and lie back down, I caught a glimpse of white material behind one of the trees a few hundred yards away. It flapped in the wind. A figure stepped out.

My breath caught in my throat.

A woman stood in the distance, surrounded by a magnificent white light. Beautiful. Every aspect of it. I didn't know her, but she looked so very familiar. I couldn't make her out a hundred percent because of the distance between us, but I knew of her long, brown hair dancing with gentle strokes in the breeze, her face like smooth porcelain and her lips lusciously full and pink.

A voice inside of me put her appearance much older than the late-twenties she looked. I couldn't explain how I knew that, I just did. She possessed a particular air about her—seasoned maturity and something else, something more... powerful. An energy buzzed in the air around me.

She edged toward me, but her movements were slow and hesitant, even though her face beamed, welcoming and pleasant. The closer she got, the more familiar she became, to the point where my eyes widened, the resemblance uncanny. She looked like...

"Elora, honey?"

Dad? Is that his voice I can hear? With my eyes still closed I couldn't tell for sure, but it sounded like him—albeit somewhat muffled and distorted.

My eyes flickered open to see Dad's tired, pale face hovering over me.

"D-dad?" I sounded hoarse, my throat dry like I'd swallowed sandpaper.

"Oh, darling, yes it's me. How are you feeling?"

"Exhausted," I croaked.

Dad's hand covered my forehead and wiped hair from my face. I struggled to remember what happened to me until Deacon's words rang through my head, 'you're bleeding!'.

"My baby... !" Trying to sit up, the sudden movement caused pain to shoot through my stomach and chest. I winced in agony and screwed my face up as I fell back against the pillows propping me up.

"Don't move, sweetheart. The baby is absolutely fine, but you need to rest."

I cupped my belly and cried. "What happened?"

"You lost some blood, darling, but you're OK now. Jacob saw to that."

"My chest... ."

"Panic attack, that's all. Nothing serious. You're gonna be fine."

Far too exhausted to try and piece anything else together, I closed my eyes again and drifted off to sleep while dad stroked my hair.

∞∞∞

Amelia and her guys spent their day trawling through yet more books. They awaited the results of the DNA samples taken from Ivy, and when night closed in, Sebastian called everybody down to his labs to discuss the evidence.

The DCI felt drained. Catching sight of herself in the reflection of the morgue's steel doors, she noted her gaunt face; pale through lack of food and proper sleep since the investigation began.

Her eyes felt hollow and the skin around them taut. But she refused to give up on the case until they found something. *Anything.* They *needed* to catch this coven before they attempted to bring any kind of demon back from the underworld.

Sam and Blake's search of the exterior of Ivy's house turned up squat. Blake suspected the sister—Madison Rose, according to letters around the house—took off through a wooded area behind the property. But her trail ran cold the moment they got past the first line of trees. Even Nate couldn't pick out any scent.

The boyfriend situation proved fruitless—nothing in the house suggested a man lived there. No male DNA, no male clothing, no letters or anything addressed to anyone other than Ivy and Madison.

The only piece of good news they did have, brought them all standing in front of Sebastian.

"I've got the results back from the DNA under Ivy's fingernails. Blood and skin particles. Her attacker was careless. No match in any of our databases, but it does match the hair you pulled from your first scene."

Amelia sighed—it didn't mean much, considering they didn't have an ID for the hair, but at least it meant the hair no longer remained circumstantial.

"You got anything else for us?" Lucas pondered.

Sebastian nodded, picking up wads of notes. "The residue from the wrists was definitely demonic. Given the extent of the damage, it was excruciatingly hot."

"Demons can't cross a salt circle, and, from what we've seen of the salt circles around our victims, they were all disturbed. Witches broke the circle, then summoned the demons to restrain our girls. What demons are we talking about here?" Amelia surmised before asking her question, certain she knew the answer.

"My team's research suggests lesser demons; ones called forth to act as servants to do the bidding of those that summon them." Sebastian shuffled the papers on the table in front of him. "They reside in the lower regions of Hell because of their inferiority and, subsequently, are one of the easiest demons to call upon."

"Are they dangerous?" Chloe's eyes bulged.

"They can be, if their instructor wills it." Amelia nodded. "They have no thought process of their own, so, they wouldn't harm you unless they were commanded to do so. And if they are, then they can be deadly."

"Where does this leave us?" Blake placed his hands on the table and glanced at Amelia.

"With a heap of information, but no actual condemning evidence," Amelia sighed.

"So what now?" he pushed.

"Now, we hope and pray that Ember gets something off that car number plate, and both Belinda Larkin and Madison Rose turn up on our doorstep alive and well... and with info on our elusive suspect."

∞ ∞ ∞

"Boss, you need to get some sleep." Sam placed his hand on Amelia's arm.

She blinked a couple of times, but her eyes remained heavy.

Chloe left for home with a mountain of paperwork to sift through, but Sam opted to stick around, offering his assistance. A fresh pair of eyes looking over all the same books and texts wouldn't hurt—even if Amelia did explain it to be a waste of time.

She ignored his statement, sat back, threw her pen down exasperatedly and sighed while she ran her hands through her hair. "This is pointless. We're going over the same shit and it's just telling us the same stuff, it isn't getting us anywhere. We know about Lilith, we know about the symbols, we know why the girls are being murdered. What we don't know is who the fucking hell is doing it, and where the hell they're hiding."

Sam blanched at Amelia's profane frustration—he'd never seen a case get under her skin in quite this way. Then again, they never encountered a supernatural case of quite an appalling nature before. Amelia was usually in top shape when it came to working these things out, but this case vexed her and it showed.

"All the more reason you need to rest. You're doing yourself no favours, Amelia."

The soft but firm use of her first name made her turn to face him.

Sam felt every bit as tired and miserable as she looked. He sympathised with how she let her emotions over this case cloud her head, but he did feel the same doubts and resignations she voiced over the situation.

Christ, they needed a break, anything to steer them in the right direction.

"Sam's right, ya know."

A gasp caught in her throat, and her body shuddered as she turned.

*

Blake leaned against the doorframe, arms folded across his chest. He stared at her and his senses came alive. Charges fired around his brain and heat pooled in his stomach.

She may look tired and worn out, but he still thought her stunning. The sleepy look in her eyes and the way her hair fell, effortlessly, over her shoulders while she looked at him, made his whole being tingle with intense desire.

"Sleeping isn't going to find us a killer."

Her voice came out low, laced with fatigue, giving it a sensuous, dreamy undertone.

"Neither is burning the candle at both ends. You have to rest, Amelia, your body needs it."

"How do you know what my body needs?" she asked, staring at him from under thick lashes.

Moving off the doorframe, he gazed at her, his breathing heavy. "It speaks to me."

"Does it now? What else does it say?"

"Ahem." Sam cleared his throat, an exaggerated sound indicating his presence. He shifted in his seat.

Amelia smirked and turned back around, but neither offered an apology. After a few more seconds she stood up.

"Fine. I'm going to bed." She turned to Blake when he growled his approval. "Alone."

His shoulders sagged. But he stiffened, attempting to hide his disappointment.

Amelia sauntered past him and he breathed her in, training his gaze on the supple skin of her smooth face. He caught her eye and held her focus while she strode out the door.

"You can put your tongue away now, Blake, buddy. I don't need to see you drooling over my boss," Sam stated once Amelia walked out of earshot.

Blake shot him a frozen look. "That obvious, huh?"

"Dude, you might as well be wearing a freakin' neon sign."

"What's her deal?"

Sighing, Sam leaned back in his chair and clasped his hands behind his head. "She's letting this case consume her. She thought she'd have it wrapped up by now, but it's moving too fast for her to come to terms with and a get a grip on."

"It's not exactly a cut and dried case, though." Blake took a seat in front of Sam.

"She doesn't see it like that. All her supernatural cases have been a breeze compared to this, and I think she was hoping it wouldn't be any different. She knew the moment she saw the first body that it was so far beyond what she's been used to. She won't let anything come between her and solving this thing."

"Not even...?"

"No, mate, sorry. She likes you, but she's scared to delve into anything in case it clouds her rational thinking."

"Then we'd better get this solved in double time, because the woman is driving me insane."

"I hear you, bro."

Blake stood, but rushed footsteps capture his attention before Amelia bolted back in.

"Ember's got a name off the vehicle," she gasped.

∞∞∞

I couldn't sleep—afraid in case something else happened to me. My last nightmare seemed so real, the pain in my chest mimicked the pain I felt when the force hit me during my dream. I needed Deacon, needed to feel his touch, his warmth, his influence.

Crawling out of bed, I decided to take a walk to calm my nerves. I put my dressing gown on and headed out the door.

Barefoot, I padded toward the living area, but slowed as I neared the door. Voices came from the other side. I thought it sounded like Amelia, and I definitely heard Deacon's voice. I quickened my pace. My heat beat faster and my stomach pitched.

I tiptoed through the doors and found Deacon sat with Amelia, Blake, and two others I didn't know. One, a man with messy brown hair, rather young-looking with tattoos and piercings.

The other, a redheaded… girl?—she looked younger than me. Vampire for sure, I could tell by her purple eyes. Her body all but dripped off Deacon's arm and my stomach lurched into my throat through pure, unadulterated jealousy. Until he shrugged her off.

He seemed irritated by her, his shoulders tense, but she appeared oblivious to it while she pawed at him.

Dressed like a hussy—short, black mini skirt, white knee-high socks with chunky, black heels and a tight-fitting, breast-enhancing white blouse—she looked every bit the part of an undead St Trinian, straight off some tacky movie set.

Deacon straightened and cocked his head before he turned to look directly at me. My heart fluttered. A sudden spark of happiness and pure delight crossed his features and his eyes dazzled, catching mine in an all-encompassing stare. I felt my face heat all over again when I returned his smile.

In a blink and miss it moment, he stood in front of me. He rubbed his hands up and down my arms. I closed my eyes against the comforting warmth.

A faint growl erupted from the sofas and I knew it came from that skanky vampire. I opened my eyes to find Deacon's gaze still on me, a gorgeous, dreamy half-smile plastered across his face.

"Couldn't sleep?"

I shook my head. "Afraid the nightmares will come back."

"Do you want me to sit with you?"

My widening eyes betrayed my approval, almost certain stars danced around them. I beamed at him. He returned my smile with one of equal affection and bent to place a gentle kiss on my forehead.

Sparks ignited. I closed my eyes and let the feelings wash over me in a refreshing torrent of pleasure and yearning.

"How cosy. A human, a vampire and a baby. Right little soap opera."

Damn vampire harlot! Why did she feel the need to open her stupid, fat, slutty mouth? *What is her problem?* Wanted Deacon and couldn't have him? Jealous tart. Right then, I wouldn't have minded if she burst into flames and burned to death right in front of my eyes.

Angry much? The hate I felt pouring off her spilled toward me in droves and I imagined myself feeding off the potency. My stomach started to heat, a fire built up inside—dancing around while the blaze licked higher and higher.

The blue flames from the pretty fireplace captured my attention. They danced about like an infusion of brightly-lit fireflies.

"Shut the hell up, Ember, it's got nothing to do with you?" Blake growled at her.

"She's a human, is all I'm saying. And she expects him to bring up another man's brat?" She pointed a finger at me, but her eyes remained on Blake.

The fire in my belly raged like someone threw petrol over it. *Brat? Did she just call my unborn child a brat?* A physical energy surged through me, my stomach bubbled and my brain sent electric pulses all through my body.

A spark from the fire jumped onto Ember's skin and ignited the sleeve of her shirt.

She jumped, screaming, and flapped at her arm with her free hand in an attempt to put the flames out. I laughed, and Deacon swapped his gaze from me to her and back again. He looked at me in shock.

It didn't take long for Ember to put out the little pyrotechnic display on her arm. She snapped her head in my direction. Her eyes glazed over and her fangs dropped before she growled at me.

"You bitch. This was my favourite blouse."

"Then I did you a favour, you trashy whore." The words left my mouth before my brain engaged them. *Where has this new attitude sprung from?*

Ember launched herself at me like a leaping gazelle before anyone could act. From behind, she grabbed me round the chest with one arm and yanked my head to the side with the other, baring my neck. Pain shot down my spine at the ferocity of her assault.

Deacon, Blake, Amelia and the brown-haired guy all shouted 'no' before she plunged her fangs into my exposed flesh.

Sharp agony pierced my senses and heat spread across my neck, and shoulders in a feverish flush.

My body reacted in a second. I felt it—so surreal. A massive wave of energy surged from my stomach and bolted straight up my chest and down my arms. My body bucked and contracted with quick, violent spasms.

I raised a hand to Ember's face, grazing her head with my fingertips. A sizzling charge shot from my palm and slammed against her forehead. She flew backward and smashed into the wall with an audible grunt. The wall cracked under the pressure and Ember coughed as dust swirled her head.

Deacon and Blake pounced on her.

I stared at the scene in front of me, while Amelia joined my side. She snaked her arm around my waist and pulled me close.

Ember lay on the floor, Deacon in her face while Blake held her down. Both of them bared their fangs, hissing and growling at Ember while she cowered beneath them. She looked scared—a true delight to see. But Deacon... he looked full of rage. Red-faced, he towered over Ember.

Warm trickles of blood oozed their way down my neck and I clamped my hand over the wounds to stem the flow.

Deacon looked up at Blake. "You and Sam get her out of here before I rip her fucking throat out."

His raised voice, with such raw emotion and authority, set my blood boiling in an entirely different way altogether. I couldn't help it. My whole body came over in goose bumps and a pleasant tingle ran all the way down my spine and exploded in my core!

Blake and Sam heaved a sobbing Ember off the floor and dragged her toward the main exit as she kicked and twisted in their grasp.

With exposed fangs, she hissed and snapped at Sam. He head-butted the idiotic vampire and her nose erupted, spraying blood down her already stained, once-white shirt.

I could hear Ember's wailing from behind the doors while they went to throw her out.

Deacon walked over to me and moved my hand away from my neck.

Vampire saliva contained healing properties—my dad told me—but even with that knowledge and the raw state my emotions were in, when Deacon trailed his delicate tongue over the holes in my neck, I struggled to hold back the orgasmic scream begging to rip from my throat.

My hand flew up to grab a tight hold on his muscular arm. My nails dug into his flesh while his tongue caressed my neck, so light it tickled, reaching the same places a lot of Deacon's actions seemed to reach. For a brief moment, I almost forgot Amelia stood beside me— until she shifted and her arm left my waist.

I pulled back from Deacon when Amelia stepped away. She looked a little embarrassed with rosy cheeks, and somewhat bewildered, which made my whole face burn, I imagine a deep shade of red.

Deacon stole my gaze for a moment. His sparkling eyes met mine and crinkled behind his smirk. I ran my fingers across the area where Ember bit me—nothing, no puncture marks, and it appeared Deacon took it upon himself to rid me of the blood that oozed down my neck.

I glanced back over at Amelia, still looking rather bemused. Deacon wore a similar expression and then it dawned on me—*what just happened here?* I didn't remove Ember's mouth from my neck by brute force, so how the hell did I do it?

Chapter 12

Amelia sat alone in her room going over what Ember discovered.

The vampire ought to thank her lucky stars no-one ordered the final death for her after a stunt like that. Laws prohibited unprovoked human attacks, only rogue vampires—those who let the bloodlust consume them—were foolish and senseless enough to attack innocents. And they paid for their crimes.

 Lucas spoke to Ember's superiors from her Faction; they would deal with her now.

Before going bat-shit crazy, Ember told them the car outside Belinda Larkin's house belonged to a woman named Laila Farris. Nothing of much interest could be found on her—no priors, no record. Amelia would send Sam and Chloe round in the morning to question her whereabouts, and why her car was seen outside a potential witness's home.

However, while the Laila Farris lead could prove fruitful, Amelia also harboured confused feelings over Elora's display of power earlier that evening. Amelia assumed Ellie fell into the 'normal human' category, but now her mind ticked over.

A knock at the door shook her from her distractions. She rose from the bed to answer it, then realised she forgot to lock it after her.

Blake opened it a fraction. "Is it safe?" he asked—she heard the smile in his voice.

"This time." She offered her own smile back.

"I just thought I'd come and see how you were after tonight's episode." He strode across to where Amelia stood by the bed in three swift paces.

Amelia could tell from his heavy-lidded gaze, his reasons for standing in front of her now did not stop at checking on her frame of mind—nothing happened to her. Blake knew she could handle herself, being a police officer strengthened her resolve for such situations, so why the fabricated excuse?

Raising her eyes to meet his, Amelia stared at him from under long lashes—her lips parted, breathing low. His warm breath swept across her, sending electrifying impulses all the way down to her aching core, the desire for him to touch her, potent.

Blake brought his hand up to her face. He traced a gentle path across her bottom lip with his thumb. If his mere touch could induce an orgasm, she would've been a quivering mess of sexual energy right now.

What the hell is happening to me? She tried to swallow when he moved his hand away. Turning instead—a distraction from his delicious stare—she bent over the bed and grabbed her papers and folders.

Blake let out a distinct, low growl. She stood up upon gathering her files. Clutching them to her chest, she turned to face him—a slight smirk danced across her face knowing she caused his carnal reaction.

"I'm fine, but that's not why you're here." She raised her eyebrows at him and walked toward the wardrobe containing her bag.

"You're right, it's not," he uttered in a low, raspy voice heavy with desire.

He stood right behind her—she could sense his body's closeness, feel the raw heat emanating from him.

"Down boy," she whispered, her back still to him.

He growled again.

Amelia reached for the handle to pull the wardrobe door open, but Blake snaked his hand around her waist and slammed it shut.

Turning to face him, files still held to her chest, she leaned back against the wood.

"I suggest, Inspector, that you watch that pretty little mouth of yours. You may be the commanding officer where your team is concerned, but making demands of me has consequences."

She got under his skin—she knew it, he knew it. She recognised the sexual connotations oozing from his words when he leaned in close.

His lips traced a feather-light caress against her ear.

Before he could open his mouth, Amelia spoke, "I love a challenge, Ace."

He pressed his body so close to her, she felt his immediate reaction—his concrete erection pressed into her thigh. She suppressed the moan caught in her throat.

He brought his face back to meet hers—his eyes stared at her parted lips. Flicking her tongue over to moisten them, she heard Blake's breathing waver.

"Blake...," she whispered, her voice shaky.

"Yeah?" he responded on a breath.

Amelia struggled with her words. She knew what she wanted to say, but felt afraid to. She desperately needed to feel the touch of his lips on hers, but she owed Blake her undivided affections. She couldn't give him that right now, her judgment, her thinking, both clouded because of the case. If anything happened tonight it would be through sheer frustration—a heat of the moment response brought on by something other than their feelings for one another.

"I can't... not yet." Amelia placed a hand on his chest.

A low rumble escaped him when he closed his eyes, resting his forehead on hers.

"I'm sorry, I want--"

He silenced her with a finger pressed gently to her lips. "I understand... I'll wait."

With a blur of flesh and fabric, he disappeared out the door.

∞∞∞

Amelia awoke the next morning feeling anything but refreshed. She opened her eyes, but didn't move for more than ten minutes while she stared at the ceiling in contemplation.

The potential suspect in their sights faded into the background; Amelia couldn't get past the previous night's events with Blake.

Excitement about Laila Farris paled in comparison, and it shouldn't—she needed to focus on the case.

She remembered Blake's reaction to her refusal, his promise to wait for her. Lust and longing hummed through her body when those words floated from his lips, full of desire. But this morning, in the cold light of day, she felt... confused, distracted.

The shrill ring of her phone stunned her to her senses. Grabbing it, she looked down at the caller—Sam.

Swiping the screen, she answered, "What's up, Chapman?"

"We may have a slight issue, ma'am."

Amelia closed her eyes and held in the frustrated sigh threatening to come out. "Yes...?"

"A Miss Laila Farris called the station this morning to report her car stolen."

"What?!" Amelia sat bolt upright. "You've gotta be kidding me."

"I wish I was, ma'am. She rang the office first thing. Reception alerted Thomas after the name rang a bell. I've just got off the phone to HQ."

The timing is one hell of a coincidence. But if it really did turn out to be car theft, and Laila's involvement with these murders happened to be wishful thinking, then she wanted to be focusing her energy into finding the next clue. "You and Roberts go interview her, see what she has to say for herself. And Chapman, I still wanna know about her whereabouts. She could be lying."

"Sure thing, ma'am. I'll call you when we're done."

Amelia hung up, threw her phone on the bed and ran her hands through her messy hair, leaning back against the headboard. *Great, just what I need*—another potential dead end.

They needed a small miracle. They needed to find Belinda and Madison Rose before the death toll mounted. She would spend her day at the station searching for any information that might suggest where Belinda and Madison Rose might be hiding—friends, relatives, colleagues, *anything.*

∞∞∞

My own company grew real old, real fast. Deacon stayed throughout the night, worrying over me after psycho vamp sank her fangs into my neck, but he left before morning to rest. Work occupied Dad's time—though he visited me again after hearing what happened. I tried to call Alice, only to be put through to voicemail. I refrained from leaving a message, though—I didn't want to worry her, I'd see her soon.

I needed somewhere other than the confines of my room to wrap my head around the events of the past couple of days—I could feel changes going on within my body, but I couldn't fathom them out at all and it drove me crazy. Not to mention it scared the crap out of me.

Walking up and down the same spot in my room, wearing holes in the plush carpet, proved to be getting me exactly nowhere.

My instructions were not to leave the premises, but dad suggested my stay here extended to the gardens housed within the Compound's huge, secured perimeter walls. If I happened to misinterpret, tough, because I needed some fresh air.

The gorgeous sun shone through the window, bright and warm, so I decided a coat unnecessary over my loose, cherry coloured, summer dress. I put a pair of white, flat pumps on, grabbed a book I borrowed from the Compound's library and waddled my way into the corridor.

I rubbed my growing belly—it felt real heavy now and I knew my little girl wouldn't be in there too much longer. It took my breath away watching the life inside me stretch and kick—I could watch for hours and still not believe a little person grew in there.

I made my way down the hall, entering the deserted, main living area. Without the staff and vamps running around like headless chickens, an eerie silence descended upon the Compound.

I headed for the stairs leading to reception and greeted Wendy with a smile she returned. Her cheeks plumped up with a beam covering most of her chubby face.

"Hiya, honey. How are you feeling today?"

Ha, a question I wondered myself. "I feel great thanks, Wendy." *Big fat lie,* "I was just hoping to get a breath of fresh air before I went stir crazy in my room. Is that OK?"

"Sure is, my sweet. There are cameras all over, so I got you covered."

Thank God, I half expected her to have been given orders not to allow me outside. The last thing I wanted was an argument with Wendy about how I am not a caged animal.

She buzzed me out of the foyer and I closed my eyes, taking deep lungfuls of actual fresh air—it felt awesome. I savoured the feel of the warm sun against my skin and the slight breeze rustling through my hair—bliss.

Opening my eyes, I saw the front gates from where I stood, two sentry towers either side of them. I looked up, but couldn't see anybody there. Maybe they were inside it somewhere, watching on monitors.

I followed the path leading around the side of the building to the gardens. I planned on sitting by one of the large ponds to lap up the sun while I got lost in my book. Only my plans were scuppered when I heard someone shout from outside the gates.

"Hey, hey you… please… can you help me?"

I jumped, even at the delicate, soft sound piercing the otherwise quiet atmosphere.

Looking over toward the huge entrance, I couldn't see anyone. I felt a bit wary as I edged a little closer, but then a girl came into view. Her hair sat on her head a bedraggled mess, her face and clothes covered in dirt and grass stains, her legs bare and equally filthy, and she wore no shoes on her bloodied feet.

"Who are you?" I took a cautious step closer.

I should've felt scared. Daniel insinuated someone other than he sought me out, and not knowing who *they* were, or what they looked like, my guard should've been up. But something in me—an ethereal voice—told me this young woman didn't pose a threat.

On closer inspection, I could see her dirty, tear-stained face, twigs and dried leaves in her hair.

"Please help me, someone is trying to kill me."

She stepped out of the shadows of the trees shielding her and when the light hit her I could see her heavily pregnant position. Before I could process anything else, a commanding voice boomed from above me.

"Stop right there or we'll shoot."

Chapter 13

The deep voice thundered over large speakers I noted above the gates, and I jumped. The woman on the other side recoiled, ready to scurry back into the woodlands she emerged from, but I think the pure fear registered across her ashen face kept her rooted.

From the bottom of one of the turrets, a man dressed in black combat gear appeared. "Stay back, miss." He held a hand out in my direction, but his blacked-out headgear restricted my view of his line of sight.

I stepped back when he made his way to the two sets of large gates. The woman trembled before him during their muted conversation. She clutched at her arms and wept.

The guard waved his hand at one of the turrets and the gates opened. Another watcher appeared from the opposite tower and, between the two of them, they escorted the terrified-looking newcomer toward the Compound.

The two men gripped an arm each and dragged her past me. She looked at me in despair, and in that split moment I guessed her to be a few years older than me, with deep purple hair and beautiful, sapphire eyes, red-rimmed and imploring me to help.

"Where are you taking me? Please, let me go. You're hurting me." The woman tried to pull back against the strength of the sentries, but they out matched her efforts and continued to pull her toward the entrance.

Rage swirled in my stomach.

"Hey, let go of her arms like that. Can't you see how terrified she is? You're not bloody helping her, you're hurting her." I stepped in, hoping they'd release their hold on her arms when a small white, electric charge flew from my fingertips and hit the man closest to me.

He let go of the woman and shook his hand, grimacing in pain.

What the hell just happened? The other guard let go of the girl in a hasty fashion.

The stranger ran and hid behind my back. Her hands gripped onto my shoulders with unexpected strength.

Turning to her, I soothed, "Hey, hey, it's OK. No-one's going to hurt you. What's your name?"

Her stare darted between me and the two men, the first of whom now grasped his hand in between his legs.

He jumped about like an idiot in an effort to stop his obvious discomfort. I questioned the expertise of the men in charge of protecting the gates, and almost scoffed in disbelief.

"They won't hurt you, don't worry. What's your name sweetheart?"

"B-Belinda ... Belinda Larkin."

She cowered in terror and I felt sorry for her, and ashamed for the way these two men manhandled her through the gates.

I glared at them. "What the hell did you think you were playing at?"

"She's a stranger, miss. She could be dangerous," the man on the left murmured.

"Does she look dangerous to you? She's petrified and, in case you both missed the obvious, she's pregnant."

The guard on the right stopped bouncing about and addressed me, "She needs to be interviewed by Lucas before she can be deemed a non-threat."

"Lucas isn't going to be available right now, so I'll talk to her. You two run along and get back to your stations, before you miss an actual threat." I turned my back on them and led Belinda toward the gardens.

"Miss, I can't allow you to do that." Guard number two put his hand on my shoulder. "She's a stranger here; she must be seen by the General."

"Feel free to wake him, then. In the meantime, we'll be in the gardens." I lifted my hand to remove his, but he wisely swiped it away himself.

I kinda liked this new bossy, confident me. I didn't know where she came from, but I found myself hoping she'd stick around.

"Very well, miss. But Hillard will have to remain with you."

With a roll of my eyes, I tutted at both men. The unnamed watcher pulled a two-way radio from his jacket and spoke into it as he walked away. Hillard stood to attention, waiting for me to make a move.

Steering Belinda to one of the large, crystal clear lakes at the back of the Compound, I motioned for her to join me sitting at the water's edge.

Hillard hung back out of earshot.

Belinda hesitated. She looked around, nervous, before her eyes settled on me.

Patting the ground beside me, I told her, "I'm not going to hurt you, Belinda. My name's Elora, can you tell me what happened to you?"

I didn't know what I expected her to say or do, but I wasn't at all prepared for her to burst into tears. She dropped to her knees and flung herself into my arms, body wracked with uncontrollable sobs. I put my arm around her shoulders and rubbed her back with my other hand.

Belinda pulled away after a long, awkward minutes. "I'm so sorry, I didn't mean to get you into trouble. I didn't know where else to go. I thought I'd be protected here."

"Protected from what, sweetie?"

"You're one of us, aren't you?"

She might've ignored my question, but now she threw me through a loop.

"One of you?" I screwed my face up—whatever did she mean?

"You're a witch."

Her simple statement floored me. My nervous laughter resonated and Belinda's expression turned uncomfortable and uneasy.

Chuckling subsiding, I asked her, "A witch? What makes you say that?"

"What you did to that guard. The power that came from your hand-- "

"It was obviously just static electricity or something. Must've given him a shock." *Wow, a quick response considering even I didn't buy it.*

Belinda looked incredulous. *Yup, she isn't buying your bull either, Ellie.* How do you explain something you haven't quite fathomed out for yourself, yet?

I let it go for the time being and reverted back to my original question. "Who do you need protection from Belinda?"

"From the witches who want my baby." She looked from her bump to mine and her mouth gaped. "Are they after you, too?"

The unfounded conclusions she kept jumping to started to scare me. My nerves were already shot.

"Who are *they*, Belinda?"

They... Daniel's words came back to haunt me like a brick to the face.

According to him, someone wanted me and my baby—I started to feel very sick. My scalp prickled and my palms began to sweat.

Belinda looked at me and cocked her head. "The witches."

"What do they want with your baby?" I swallowed my fear. I didn't want to ask, but I couldn't ignore the feeling in my stomach. My skin turned clammy and nausea swept over me in fresh waves.

Belinda looked at me, with one sceptical brow raised, but then her expression turned to one of shocked realisation. I think she finally understood I didn't have the first clue. She stared at me, white-faced, but remained silent.

"Belinda, please, tell me… ." My voice quaked with desperation and terror. I needed to piece things together, but the notions were absurd and my brain refused to make any connections through stubborn fear.

Belinda started to shake through tears and I knew I'd get nothing more out of her—she needed to see Lucas and I hoped he would be able to give me some answers, too.

She thought me a witch, but why?

Something I couldn't explain told me danger lurked around the corner. It left a sickness swirling in my stomach I found impossible to ignore.

∞∞∞

Belinda watched from the bed while I paced my room. She looked contemplative yet lost, and I did take a second or two to wonder what must be going through her head, before I returned to my own inner turmoil.

Question after question scoured my mind, but my brain didn't want to accept any of them. It would mean something huge for me, but, more importantly, for my child.

I shuddered, and cupped a hand around my swollen belly. Belinda's expression changed; sympathy and knowing shadowed her soft features while her dewy-eyed gaze followed my hand.

I needed to know more; my mind reeled. I'd explode at some point unless I got answers—*any* answers.

I turned my attention to Belinda in the hopes her initial distress had subsided, asking, "So, you're a witch?"

My obvious, foolish question caused a slight smile to break Belinda's otherwise sombre appearance as she met my stare. "Yes."

"Why do you think I'm a witch?" The question I dreaded asking most, still afraid to receive the same answer.

"Because of the power you displayed earlier, with those guards. It's strong; I can feel it buzzing from you."

Buzzing? I cast my eyes up and thought about that sensation for a moment. When I couldn't recall it, my brain switched back to the moment at hand. I wanted to make up an excuse for it again, but in my heart, I knew I'd be lying to myself more than anyone else.

The episode with Ember—no-one mentioned it since, but we were being watched so I *know* everyone saw—why keep quiet about it? They knew something. If they did, I wished to God someone would tell me because my mind, my body, couldn't handle much more. Things were moving far too fast and my brain's delicate condition couldn't keep up.

Belinda nodded at me as though she could read my anxiety—certain she could sense my inner battle. I needed a distraction, but to get it while there were still unanswered questions seemed impossible. Where did I start?

I would wait until Lucas arrived—surely he would know something. Or at least have the means to find out more.

I still wanted to know more from Belinda, though. "Why are witches after your baby, when you're a witch too?"

Belinda drew herself up on the bed and tucked her legs close to her chest. I followed suit.

"Do you know anything about the practice of witchcraft?" she asked me.

I shook my head.

"Well, you have your white witches and you have your black witches. I am a white witch. The magic I practice is only used from and for good. Black witches are the complete opposite. They use their gifts for evil and destruction."

"And it's black witches that want your child?" I deduced.

"Yes."

"But why?"

"I can't be exactly sure, but there is no way I am going to let them take him." Belinda caressed her swollen belly.

"How do you know it's black witches that are after you?"

"I've met the High Priestess. I hadn't realised she practiced dark magic when she first introduced herself to us."

"Us?"

Belinda hung her head and a tear slipped down her cleaned-up face.

"I'm sorry. I didn't mean to upset you," I placed a hand on her shoulder.

"It's OK, you didn't." She looked back up at me, her eyes full of sorrow and fear.

My heart ached for whatever torment she went through.

"There have been three more before me and… ." She broke down in tears again.

Her body trembled so much I realised it couldn't have just been through sadness—*she is terrified of something.*

"It's OK, you don't have to say anything else, if it's too painful for you." I did feel like a bit of a bitch to have caused this reaction, but I really hoped she still wanted to continue with her story—I *needed* to know.

"No, I'm sorry. I just can't quite believe that it's come to this."

I tilted my head, confused for a moment.

With gentle strokes over her stomach, she elaborated, "I was told I was infertile. I couldn't have children. Then I met Cassandra and she told me she had the answer to my prayers."

"Cassandra?"

"The High Priestess. The leader of the coven."

Coven, witches, Priestesses. I knew all this existed, to a degree, but to hear it all out loud, and to even entertain the notion that it somehow might be related to me, that I might be ... *it's absurd.*

"How did she know you couldn't get pregnant?"

"I joined a support group about eighteen months ago for those who suffered from infertility. I'd always known about my gift, and it turned out one of the other women in my group was also a witch. We bonded, and eventually she asked me to be a part of Cassandra's Coven of The Beautiful Maiden. She introduced me to Cassandra."

"You said there were others before you?" My words were careful, soft—I could tell this recollection didn't come easy to a glassy-eyed Belinda. I didn't want her to break down on me when I felt I might be getting somewhere, even with my own thoughts and feelings being tested.

"That's right. There were nine of us in total, including me and Cassandra. There were three other women within the coven there under similar circumstances, and we struck up a close friendship."

"They were all infertile before Cassandra?"

"Yes, for one reason or another."

"So, what happened? How did she help you get pregnant?" My mouth went dry, I could feel a bitter taste at the back of my throat.

"I have Endometriosis. There is no cure or treatment, but Cassandra said she could change all that. All I had to do was take some herbal remedy she concocted and I'd be pregnant within a few weeks." Her voice reduced to a quivering whisper.

I almost scoffed at the thought, but I thought better of it, given Belinda's tears. Her eyes shone red and puffy and I could see she wanted to cry again.

"No need for a man?" I asked instead, unconvinced, although I tried to hide it.

"Apparently not," she stroked her belly again, and a slight smile broke across her otherwise grave expression. "I'm still a virgin."

Wow, immaculate conception... kind of. "What was it she gave you?"

Belinda looked back up at me. "I don't know. She never said, but I was willing to try anything for a baby. I've dreamed of being a mother for as long as I can remember."

I knew that feeling. The moment the doctor told me about my little princess, my heart almost burst with pride and happiness. My life would be complete when I held her in my arms, but to watch her grow inside me... I welled up at the memory. My life came together the moment I saw that positive line; my purpose clear.

I would cherish every moment I spent with her; teach her things my mum never got the chance to teach me. I would love her with everything in me and I would protect her until my dying breath. For someone to take her from me would send my world crashing down around me, in a million fiery pieces. I would become unstoppable; a reckless force hell bent on destruction. I would *kill* whoever dared put her life in jeopardy.

"Are you OK?" Belinda's hand hovered over my own. "Your body's buzzing... " She looked to the side of her.

Following her gaze, I gasped when my eyes locked on one of the bedside lamps. It lay on the floor, the metal base in pieces.

"I-I don't know, what... ."

Belinda placed her hand on mine and smiled. "It's alright. You have nothing to be afraid of."

Pot. Kettle. Black. Belinda happened to be just as frightened as I, only she knew more than I did.

Though my body trembled, I tried to gather my thoughts, still staring at the shattered pieces of a solid metal lamp. *I did that?* With my mind? Jesus, I couldn't even begin to work it out. I needed a distraction, yet everywhere I turned, every question I asked, every new one that formed... I couldn't escape the cold, hard reality of my situation. I needed more information, and yet I didn't want to hear anymore.

But I couldn't run from it. It would catch up with me and knock me down flat on my face if I ignored it.

I resumed our conversation, "What makes you think these witches are after you now?" I tore my eyes away from the lamp, half-dreading Belinda's response when the colour drained from her face and her body sagged.

She stole her gaze away from mine as tears slipped down her face. "The other three women; my friends, they're all dead now."

Chapter 14

Amelia came up empty at the station; a search on Belinda uncovered no known relatives. A senile grandma proved to be the only remaining family of Ivy and Madison Rose, and she resided in a nursing home for Alzheimer's sufferers—a phone call to the establishment provided Amelia with no further information.

Putting her elbows on her desk and her forehead in her hands, she let out an exasperated sigh before her door burst open, and her intruder waltzed into her office, unannounced and uninvited.

In a deep, brusque voice DCS Thomas Riley asked, "Ellis, what's the latest?"

Running her hands through her hair, she looked up at the imposing, bulky figure of her boss. *He would be perfect in some Hell's Angels gang*, with his bald head and trimmed, grey flecked, brown beard. His pale blue eyes bore into her while he waited for an answer.

She kept her answer brief and to the point, "Three murders. Two missing, potential witnesses and one potential suspect. Though she may be ruled out tod--"

"How so?" he interrupted.

Riley would have this information, but the expectant look across his face told Amelia he edged to find out what she knew, but more importantly, he wanted her take on it.

"Laila Farris's car was outside a witness's house and disappeared after we were attacked and the intruder fled. Next thing we know, Farris reports her car stolen and, pardon my bluntness sir, but that smells like a crock of shit to me."

"So, what are you doing about it?"

"Chapman and Roberts are round there now to get all the details, and question her whereabouts for all three murders."

"Do we have a timeframe for these murders?"

"T.O.D suggests it happened within hours of the bodies being discovered, sir."

"What are you left with if Farris's story adds up?"

"Two missing witnesses we're doing everything to locate." Amelia's mobile rang at that moment—the Compound. She answered it without an apology to her boss.

"DCI Ellis... Hello, Wendy... Yes... WHAT?! ... I'll be right over."

"Good news, I hope?" Thomas raised a brow.

"One of the witnesses, Belinda Larkin, she's just turned up at the Compound."

Amelia didn't give Thomas chance to say another word; she grabbed her jacket and flew out of her office.

∞∞∞

Flooring her car, Amelia made it to the Compound in record time and slammed the brakes on outside the building. She grabbed her files and exited the car. Using her newly acquired ID pass, she entered through the main gates.

Affording Wendy a quick wave, Amelia all but fell into the elevator. She tapped her foot, files clutched against her chest as she drummed her fingers on her crossed arms. A knot built in her stomach at the anticipation of finally getting a lead on this case.

She didn't wait for the elevator doors to open all the way before she ambled out and into the large living room.

A subdued atmosphere welcomed Amelia into the darkened living space—the blinds drawn against the penetration of natural light. Hushed voices were emphasised by the lack of music, but they died down when Amelia walked in.

Lucas stood by the fireplace and Nate sat on one of the sofas. Elora sat opposite with Belinda—Amelia assumed—beside her.

She wondered about Elora's presence for a moment.

"Hey, beautiful." Nate smiled at her, oozing his usual charm.

She forced a smile back, but avoided any small talk, eager to find out what transpired during her absence. She directed her gaze straight at Lucas in an effort to get him to start talking.

He held a hand out to the stranger, "Amelia, this is Belinda Larkin."

Glancing over, she noted the young, tired, pale woman. Her deep purple hair did nothing for her pallor, nor the dark circles under her eyes. The quick introduction out the way, Amelia sat and took the lead.

"Hi, Belinda, I'm Amelia. Can you tell me where you've been since you contacted us?"

Belinda shifted her gaze to Elora, who in turn offered a reassuring nod.

"I've been using the cover of the woods to make my way here."

Amelia nodded with a gentle smile. "You said you think you're the next target?" She continued after Belinda's quick nod, "Can I ask why you think that?"

Belinda proceeded to tell Amelia about her time in Cassandra's mansion and the gathering of her and her friends elsewhere. She described the witches best she could, telling the DCI about the rituals and the pregnancies. Amelia listened, while Nate scribbled down notes beside her.

"Belinda, can you tell me the names of the other three women."

"Yeah. Morgan, Gillian, and Ivy."

"And how did you know the other witches had been murdered?"

Belinda dropped her sheepish gaze to the floor. "I had a premonition of their deaths."

Elora looked at Belinda with wide eyes.

Amelia didn't say anything straight away. From experience, Belinda's submissive body language told her she kept something back. Guilt marred her face. Her eyes said as much when she squeezed them closed.

Opening them, she told Amelia, "I saw it happen before it did, and I did nothing to stop it," before she burst into tears.

Ellie put an arm around her shoulder and held her close.

Amelia felt sorry for this woman—the ordeal she must've gone through didn't bare thinking about, and given the state of the crime scenes, Amelia awarded her credit for having held it together this long.

"Do you think there was anything you could've done?" she asked Belinda in a gentle tone.

Belinda's crying subsided to quivering sniffles while she composed herself. "I could've warned them. I could've warned *you* sooner."

"Can you describe to me what you saw in your visions?"

"My dreams aren't always clear. I-I saw people with milk-white eyes, in brown robes hovering above me. Blood dripped down their chins." Her voice lowered to a sobbing whimper while her body shook. "M-my wrists and ankles began to burn and I tried to move them, but I couldn't... I just couldn't.

"When I opened my mouth to scream, nothing came out. One of the... one of *them*, they sliced my stomach open with a knife and took my baby from me, while I died on the cold floor of some dirty warehouse."

Elora let out a gasp and her hand flew to her mouth, her eyes widened. Having witnessed the terror first-hand, Amelia understood her shock at the brutality.

"You couldn't have done anything, Belinda. To you, it probably seemed like a nightmare you were having. How could you possibly have known?"

Belinda's cries grew louder and she shook her head. "I-I knew... I knew something was wrong. I've had visions before. I can feel and sense things I shouldn't be able to. I could've stopped this."

No blame lay with Belinda, but Amelia felt her anguish. The images—the horror, the pain, the fear—made the guilt understandable.

"There was no way for you to know who you were dreaming about, Belinda."

"I still should've known... ." Belinda broke off into uncontrollable sobs, the rest of her words incoherent.

Elora, paling visibly, clasped her tighter and pulled her in, trying to soothe away the pain. Amelia didn't know what else to say to the inconsolable witch.

Belinda's crying abated when she looked back at Amelia. "I should've known better when I had my second vision."

∞ ∞ ∞

It didn't matter how many times Amelia told Belinda not to blame herself, the woman wouldn't listen.

She described her second premonition—a similar death, the outright fear of the victim, the house, the room, the moment the murderer approached her with a knife. Amelia asked her to describe the knife, and she explained it looked to be made from bone, with a corked handle and feathers around the hilt.

During the description, Lucas noticed Elora's face drain of whatever colour remained. She excused herself when Belinda's described dreaming of a clearing in a storm-riddled forest.

He harboured his own thoughts for why Elora turned a ghastly shade of white before she bolted—he could *sense* the emotions pouring from her and they weren't just from shock—fear radiated from her in droves.

A few moments of silence followed before Belinda pulled herself together. Elora walked back into the room looking gaunt and full of anguish. She shuffled back to the sofa and sat. She didn't make eye contact with anyone, but stared at the floor with her hands fisted in her lap. Lucas noted her red-rimmed, puffy eyes.

Letting his suspicions subside for the moment, he listened while Nate went to fetch water and tissues.

Amelia continued to question Belinda. "Belinda, can you tell us a bit about Cassandra. What she was like, how she treated you, that sort of thing?"

Belinda thanked Nate for the tissue and dabbed it around her moist eyes. "To start with, she was lovely, she made me feel like I wasn't... different. When I found out about my condition, I was beside myself with grief. For months I moped around not really living, just existing, until a card got pushed through my door one day. A support group for infertility. I'd been praying to the Goddesses for a sign and that was it.

"I went to the group the next night. I met Serena there; she belonged to Cassandra's coven and told me chemotherapy left her infertile. She seemed so nice and understanding, said she had hope. I asked her if the support group gave her that hope, but she told me it was Cassandra.

"Serena told me that within months of meeting Cassandra, she had fallen pregnant—even showed me pictures of her baby. So, I asked her why she still came and she said to give courage and faith to other young witches like me."

"And so, you went to see Cassandra?" Amelia urged with a sympathetic tone.

"Not right away, I was sceptical, at first. It took me another couple of weeks of therapy until I decided I was strong enough to meet her. I'd been too scared to dream in case it didn't work. If that happened, I wouldn't have been able to cope. But I knew just talking about my feelings in group wasn't going to get me what I wanted, so I told Serena to take me to Cassandra.

"She took me to a big, gothic mansion where Cassandra introduced herself to me. She was warm and friendly, and she didn't show me pity like everyone else. She told me she wanted to help, if it was what I wanted. I wanted it so badly, I almost begged her on the spot."

Belinda paused again to wipe more tears from her eyes with her crumbling tissue.

Amelia gave her another. "Take your time, Belinda. When you're ready, tell us what happened after you joined Cassandra's coven."

The witch shifted and straightened her back. After a deep breath, she continued, "It was strange. It wasn't like most covens I know of."

"How do you mean?" Amelia leaned forward and placed her arms on her legs, intertwining her fingers.

"Well, a coven is usually made up of around thirteen witches, although that number isn't as significant this day and age. But usually you have your High Priestess, then you would usually have a High Priest, a Summoner and a Handmaiden. Cassandra never introduced the other witches present as any of those, so to be missing those people seemed odd to me."

"I suspect she wasn't offering you a position in a coven, Belinda. She was using other black witches to form a cult of sorts, in order for her to fulfil her purpose."

"What purpose?"

"We think she's trying to raise Lilith," Nate interjected, before Amelia could reply.

The DCI rolled her eyes at him.

"Lilith? That's ridiculous. Lilith is just a myth, how can they possibly think they can kill children to raise someone who doesn't exist." Belinda's voice took on an angry inflection and her brow creased.

"They seem to have a different perspective, and they're sacrificing babies in order to reach their goal."

"Jesus." Belinda breathed out. "I thought they were crazy, but I didn't think they were *that* crazy."

"What do you mean?" Amelia asked.

"During what they classed as 'prayers', they would stand naked in a circle, chanting, and expect us to do the same. They cut themselves and bled into this horrific looking chalice carved from bone. We all had to drink from it."

Nate gagged. "That's disgusting. Has no one ever heard of Hep C?! Or even Aids for that matter."

Amelia glared at him, a rigid look saying 'shut the hell up', which he promptly did.

"I can't describe it any better than by saying my body didn't feel like I had control over it. I could see what they were doing and I could register my own revulsion, but I couldn't stop myself from taking part in the rituals. Cassandra promised it was all necessary for us to fall pregnant; for her remedy to eventually work."

"So, she hadn't given you the remedy at that point?" Amelia inquired.

"Not when all that first began. But even after she gave it us, we still had to drink each other's blood."

"What was in the remedy she gave you?"

"I don't know, but it tasted of a mixture of things. It was sweet and flowery, but it also tasted quite earthy as well, and it was thick and oily."

"Sounds delicious." Nate's lips dipped at the corners in a grimace.

"I wasn't concerned with the taste if it meant I would get pregnant." Bitterness laced Belinda's tone. She stared at Nate, who avoided her gaze, looking somewhat ashamed for his unnecessary comment.

"What happened next, Belinda?" Amelia cast Nate another knitted glance that could turn any normal person to stone.

"That went on for a couple of weeks. We kept up with the prayers, the blood drinking and some other ritual Cassandra said would aid fertility. After those weeks, the three of us fell pregnant within days of one another. We couldn't believe it." Belinda smiled for a brief moment, stroking her belly.

Placing his arms on his knees, Nate clasped his hands in front of him. "What happened between that time and the time the first victim was murdered?"

"Morgan. Your first *victim* was Morgan." Belinda sighed before continuing, "Things were still the same. We still had to drink the remedy on a daily basis, we still chanted naked and drank blood, although not as often. I found it strange we didn't practice magic like I expected we would. Morgan, Gillian, Ivy and I sometimes stayed at Cassandra's, but we'd often get together ourselves and practice. Usually when no one else was around."

"Ivy was found at her home, but Morgan and Gillian were found elsewhere. Why was that?" Amelia quizzed.

Belinda paused and swallowed hard. "When we weren't at Cassandra's we stayed in touch with one another. We would meet up in abandoned warehouses to practice and pray. It was easier to go there from our homes after we started getting bigger. But Ivy struggled to get around after a while, so we stopped until after we… until we gave birth."

Amelia handed Belinda another tissue when fresh streams trailed down her face. "Where does Cassandra live?" She slipped her hand to Belinda's knee.

Between sniffles, Belinda replied, "Somewhere outside of Simonstone. A place called Huntroyde Hall, I think."

Elora stifled another gasp and Lucas saw her eyes widen when she left out a long breath. She turned ashen and swallowed hard.

Nate resumed his straight posture. "How did Cassandra take it when you started congregating without them?"

"I don't know. She never actually came right out and said she knew we did it, but I suspected she did. She became a little more distant from us, as did the others, but we thought nothing of it. We were quite content to do what we were doing, and happy to be away from what... *they* were doing."

"You said there were three others aside from Cassandra and Serena, do you know their names?" Amelia chimed back in.

"I know the other two, but the third didn't really have much to do with us, and we weren't introduced to her. She passed around the chalice and knives, but I never saw her partake in any of it other than to drink from the strange looking cup, then she'd leave."

"What were their names?" Amelia sucked in a breath and held it.

Belinda thought for a moment, eyes focused on a spot near the fire, "Serena Dobson, Keira Hoult and Laila Farris."

Chapter 15

Belinda answered Amelia and Nate's questions best she could, but while I hoped she could help, I needed to get away; her revelations floored me.

The first mention of her dream had me running from the room to be sick. I *know* Lucas noticed my sudden departure, and not for the reasons the others must've thought. The moment Belinda finished her story, I bolted back to my room and locked myself in.

My emotions tore through me – part of me knew I should voice my opinion; *it's too much of coincidence.* The police needed to catch this killer. Lives were in danger, and innocent ones had already been lost. But what I happened to be wrong? I couldn't make sense of any connection between Daniel and Cassandra, what if the knife and the mansion meant nothing even close. I could be condemning an innocent man.

I scoffed at my own musings. Daniel was hardly an innocent man.

Pacing the bedroom once again, I stilled. I sensed a presence outside the door—I felt the hesitation, the trepidation, as though they were my own emotions.

Deciding to face this head on, I didn't wait for a knock; I opened the door to find Lucas staring at me. His jaw-length, dark hair fell around his handsome, firm-set face, but he didn't look angry, just... expectant.

I stepped aside and he entered the room, turning to look at me. Standing rigid, his muscles rippled through his black shirt when he clasped his hands behind his back. His glare unnerved me. I shied away, but I knew I couldn't keep him waiting.

"I have something I need to tell you," I blurted out.

"I figured as much." A slight smile drew across his expression; it put me at ease, sort of.

Christ, where do I even start with something like this? Lost for words, I tried to figure out what to lead with. Whatever came out my mouth would not be anything near intelligent or thought about, so I blabbed out the first thing to spring to mind.

"I think I'm a witch."

Lucas' facial features remained impassive while he moved over to the sofa. "Come and take a seat. We need to have a chat."

I shuffled over like a naughty school girl reprimanded by the headmaster. "I'm sorry... I didn't mean... what I meant was--"

"It's OK, Ellie. You're not in any trouble. For what it's worth, I think you're right, but we need to discuss the ramifications of what you're saying."

I breathed a quivering sigh of relief—if you could call it that—and sat down beside him, shaking like a nervous child. He studied me for a few seconds, but I became edgy under his gentle scrutiny.

"Am I a target?" I blurted out. I needed to settle my nerves and my mind once and for all.

"A target for what?"

Oh come on. "You know what, Lucas. I know you saw my reaction to Belinda's story."

"Her visions...?"

"... Are similar to my dreams."

"And the knife...?"

"... The same as the one I found in Daniel's car."

Lucas took a deep breath, "You think he's involved somehow?"

"Do you?"

A reluctance to admit I may have been living with a murderer circled my brain. I carried his child; it didn't bear thinking about... those atrocities. Could Daniel do something like that? How could I have been so blind?

Lucas interlaced his fingers under his chin, "I think he might be, yes. How involved, though, I don't know."

"Cassandra's home... I think he might have sold it her."

"What makes you say that?"

I told Lucas about Daniel's occupation, and how I overheard several of his conversations concerning complications with a property in Simonstone. Unfortunately, my knowledge of property development and planning permission fell much shorter than what I would have liked—I couldn't tell Lucas much more besides.

Lucas absorbed it all, inching closer with each snippet. I didn't like the worried expression forming on his rugged features. My stomach somersaulted and I felt sick all over again.

"We'll get someone to look into him right away."

Is that all you have to say? I wanted reassurances suggesting I bordered on paranoia, that the father of my child didn't go around murdering women and sacrificing their babies. That perhaps the notion of me being a witch didn't exist anywhere beside my over-active imagination.

I'd likely not buy a word of it, but I needed someone to tell me my child and I would be safe from murderous, psychotic witches.

My body shook.

Lucas left and I couldn't fight it any longer—I ran to the toilet and threw up.

∞ ∞ ∞

The moment Amelia heard Laila's name, she pulled her phone out and called Sam. Neither he nor Chloe knew about Belinda. In all the excitement to gain the upper-hand, she forgot to inform them.

"Ma'am, I was just about to call you--"

"Get back to Farris, Chapman and arrest her. She's involved in this. You need to bring her in right away."

"What's going on?"

"Belinda's here and she's named Laila. I'll explain later, just get back there and arrest her on suspicion of murder; we'll hash out the details later. Bring her straight to the Compound."

Sam's voice cut off when Amelia ended the call.

Turning to Nate, she instructed him to show Belinda to a room, and then see if he could find an address for Serena and Keira—someone needed to pay them a visit. She'd do it herself, but right now Cassandra took priority. She'd leave a message for Lucas with Wendy, then head out to grab Darcy from the station for back-up.

Almost forgetting her manners, she turned to thank Belinda for her information and cooperation. Grabbing Belinda's damp hand, Amelia held onto it for a few minutes while she looked the witch in the face, her eyes registering a smile of thanks. Belinda returned her smile as tears trickled down her face.

"I hoped I've helped this time," she whispered.

Amelia nodded, then left.

*

Nate showed Belinda to a room before he went in search of a computer to track down Keira and Serena. Seating himself at a machine in the labs, he began his search.

Lucas came over to him not long after. He looked anxious, a distinct note of urgency in his demeanour.

"Nate, I need you to run a search for me on Daniel Compton."

Nate screwed his face up in confusion. "Elora's ex nut-job?"

"Yes, he could be involved. Where's Amelia?"

"She's gone to question Cassandra."

Lucas averted his gaze and took a deep breath. "Whatever you find on Daniel, call me before *anyone* else, OK?"

"Sure thing, boss."

Lucas stalked off, leaving Nate to continue his extended search.

∞∞∞

Amelia struggled to breathe properly through her exhilaration—they were getting somewhere, she could feel it. If she could get her hands on Cassandra, things would be perfect. If she could get Laila and the ring leader into custody at the Compound, she felt certain the other two wouldn't get far, regardless of their current location.

The third unknown concerned her—no name or description. Even though Cassandra led the group of loonies, this stranger would still be dangerous; they needed to apprehend her, too. But first things first—Cassandra.

She jumped when her phone rang. Hooking it up to her hands free kit, she connected the call. "Ellis."

"Ma'am, it's Chapman. Laila's gone."

"What?!"

"We turned back around after your call. We weren't even ten minutes away, but there was no one home."

Amelia banged on the steering wheel. "Shit!"

"Sorry ma'am. We tried to get back as fast as we could."

"It's not your fault. Get back to the Compound and help Nate. Fingers crossed we get lucky." She didn't feel lucky as she disconnected Sam's call.

Familiar doubts crawled under Amelia's skin. *Where are they all? Cassandra's perhaps?* She pushed her foot harder on the accelerator. The sooner she got to Huntroyde Hall, the better.

Breaking every speed limit possible, Amelia made it back to the station in record time. She launched herself from the car and ran to grab a waiting Darcy. Bursting through the station doors, she sprinted up the stairs toward her office and collided with the Constable at the top.

"Steady, ma'am, where's the fire?" Darcy righted herself against the stair banister and smoothed out her blonde bob.

"Now's not the time, Simms, we need to get to Cassandra's quick as possible."

"Ready when you are."

Amelia grabbed hold of Darcy's arm and hauled her down the stairs two at a time—no way would she allow another witch to run out on her if she could help it.

An afternoon downpour left the roads to Cassandra's in a treacherous condition. A car had lost control in the weather, skidded ahead and landed side on. It blocked one side of the road, causing traffic to come to a standstill. It would take hours to get to Cassandra's at this rate. Their twenty minute journey already eked out to a little over ninety minutes.

Amelia's patience wore thin, her disposition black like the weather. She drummed her fingers on the steering wheel, half tempted to put the blues and twos on, but it would only succeed in driving her insane, rather than any further forward. No-one could get through on the other side—the narrow lane could barely fit one car, never mind two abreast.

She slumped her head against the chair rest and sighed. "God damn it, why now?"

Darcy cast her a half-smile, anxiously fidgeting with her fingers.

The sooner they got to Cassandra's, the better they would feel. Amelia knew her driving could be precarious at the best of times and, although they were stationary now, she'd be flooring the car at the first opportunity. It made everyone who rode with her uneasy.

Amelia caught glimpses of Darcy checking her phone every so often—*it won't make time go any faster.* Another half hour went by according to the dashboard clock. Amelia focused on the incessant green flashing of the colons between the numbers—there, gone, there, gone, there... a car horn behind them made her jump out of her trance.

Moving again, Amelia approached a turning where she could head off onto a two lane road. Wasting no time, she flicked on the siren, took the corner like her life depended on it and raced up the road. Darcy grabbed hold of the door handle and straightened against her seat. Five or so more minutes and they'd be there.

The first clap of thunder resonated over the skies and the heavens burst open, releasing fresh torrents of fat, heavy rainfall. Windscreen wipers going ten to the dozen, Amelia made out the outline of Cassandra's house coming into view. She whipped the car up the lane and attempted to park the closest she could to the front door.

The door to Cassandra's home swung ominously on its hinges, and she felt an overwhelming sense of dread, and déjà vu.

"Simms, call for back up."

Darcy attempted to call through on her radio, but got a loud hiss of static in response.

"Damn. Ma'am, I think the storm's interfering with the radios," she stated.

"Phone?" Amelia still glared at the mansion, watching for any sign of movement.

Darcy fumbled with the Velcro on her vest. "No signal," she informed after a brief pause.

"Shit!" Amelia ran her hand through her hair, then checked her own phone—no signal. "For the love of God. OK, fine. Let's go do this."

Letting out a heavy sigh, she threw the car door open, slammed it shut behind her and ran fast, toward the porch.

Reaching the porch in seconds, her light, black blazer and deep crimson shirt stuck to her body. Hair plastered her neck and she attempted to pull thick, wet strands off it and her face. She delved into her pocket and grabbed a hair tie, scrunching her tresses up into a messy ponytail. Grabbing some grips also—smiling at her intuition, never knowing when she'd have to tie her hair back during a scene visit—she clipped a few loose strands out of the way of her eyes.

Swinging round at the constable's screech, Amelia watched Darcy race at high speed toward her, head down and arms up in a failed attempt to shield herself from the pounding rain.

Giggling at both their misfortune, Amelia turned to enter the property. Something heavy smashed against her head. Stars burst into view and a hot trickle dribbled down her face before a black veil stole her conscious mind.

Chapter 16

Lucas met Sam and Chloe back in the living area at the Compound, he informed them of Amelia's visit to Cassandra's and all Elora and Belinda had divulged.

"Small world," Sam quipped, rewarding him an elbow to the ribs off Chloe.

"I've had Nate delve into Daniel's background, just as a precaution."

"Has he got anywhere yet?" Chloe queried.

By sheer coincidence, Lucas' piercing ringtone evaded the otherwise serene sounds of the music in the main quarters.

"Nate, what have you got?"

Lucas' eyes widened. He ended the call and beckoned Sam and Chloe to follow him to the labs.

Nate sat at the far end, face very nearly buried in the computer screen, studying. Lucas strolled over to him in a matter of strides and placed his hand on Nate's shoulder.

"What is it, Nate?"

Without taking his eyes off the screen, he answered Lucas's question, "I'm not sure how pertinent this is, but Daniel's father was murdered about seventeen years ago. The case is still unsolved.

"He and his father were up in some cabin his family owned; fishing I believe. His mother was an in-home caregiver, working at the time. She gave a statement saying she returned to her Burnley home some time before four in the afternoon and, afterwards, made her way to the family's lodge in Wrea Green. Upon approaching the property, she noticed the door ajar and when she entered, she saw her son, Daniel, covered in blood sitting next to the body of his dead father.

"It goes on to say that Isobel Compton found her husband, William, with multiple stab wounds to the stomach, chest, face and neck. She screamed and cradled his dead body, then she called the police."

"Sounds horrific," Chloe commented before Nate resumed his story.

"Further digging led me to a patient file. Daniel refused to speak after his father's death and attended therapy sessions for several years; he started talking again around aged thirteen. His therapist's name was George Hall, and a search on his name led me to another article, this time about *his* murder. I've printed it all off for you, there's a few grainy pictures of a young Daniel and his parents at that time, as well as one of the therapist."

"The therapist was murdered?" Lucas exclaimed.

Nate nodded. "Yeah. Stabbed outside his office as he was leaving one night."

"Coincidence?" Sam posed.

"Possibly, possibly not. I need to get a hold of those files from his sessions with Daniel," Nate explained.

"I'll look into it," Lucas started, "while you and Sam head to that cabin and see if he's hiding there. We know he's skipped out on us, so maybe he's there somewhere if his family still owns it."

Searching the property titles for Wrea Green, Lucas dug up a cabin under the name Compton. Nate grabbed the address and he and Sam took off on the sixty minute round trip. Lucas hoped they'd come back with at least some information or, with luck on their side, a disgruntled ex-partner hell bent on kidnapping a child from her mother.

In the meantime, Lucas instructed Chloe to sift through anything else that might give them more clues surrounding Daniel's past. With Chloe occupied, he tried to gain access to Daniel's patient files during the time of his therapy with George Hall.

Some twenty minutes later, Lucas turned toward heavy footsteps, seeing Deacon appear beside him.

Placing a hand on the General's shoulder, he asked, "Why are you doing a search on Daniel?" His creased brow lined with curious confusion.

The moment Lucas informed him Elora suspected she might be a witch, Deacon's eyes bulged.

"Surely you suspected." Lucas speculated.

Nodding, Deacon verified, "I did, but it's still shocking to hear someone else confirm it."

Lucas told him of his reservations over Daniel's involvement, and if Elora happened to be a witch, she would likely be a target.

"Witches are usually born of other witches, so we need information on Ellie's mother." Deacon offered.

"Do you know her name?" Lucas asked him.

Despite knowing Bernie for several years, not once could Lucas recall the mention of his wife's name.

Deacon shook his head. "I'll go ask her now." A smile flittered across his face, despite the sombre circumstances.

He left the labs bound for her room, while Lucas continued his search for Daniel's therapy files.

Fingers hovering over the keyboard, the piercing tone of his mobile phone cut through the concentration.

"General Drake."

Chloe looked up at the sound of his voice and Lucas' stared, unblinking. He told the caller someone would be right over.

"What's up?" Chloe stopped typing.

"That was Madison Rose--"

"No shit?! Ivy's sister?" She stood and her chair clattered to the floor behind her. "What did she say?"

Lucas shook his head at her animated outburst. "She has video evidence from the night her sister was murdered. You need to go and pick her up. Now. We've got no time to waste."

Clambering over her fallen chair, she ran for the door before Lucas called her back to retrieve the address she forgot in her haste. He handed her a piece of paper with directions.

"Hurry," he urged her.

∞∞∞

I couldn't escape the familiar sick feeling in my stomach. I swallowed down bile while I lay on my bed, my legs refusing to acknowledge their existence as part of my body. I felt drained, beyond exhausted.

After Lucas left, and I emptied the contents of my stomach into the toilet, I lay down and tried to wrap my head around the situation. A headache formed as the only reward for my efforts.

Pained hummed through my head when I sat up. I reached for a glass of water, taking a few, small sips. The thumping subsided—albeit only slightly—and I recalled my earlier question to Lucas. If I happened to be a witch, my 'magic abilities'—and I used the term very lightly—would have presented before now, wouldn't they? And if not, why not?

I couldn't deny the strange things happening to me. The shock I gave the guard, the super charged bolt I bounced off Ember's head—I smiled—and the unexplained feelings and sensations rushing through my body during emotional episodes; my heightened senses, time slowing down, far off noises only audible to my ears.

Did my emotions have to be put through the ringer in order for my... powers to manifest? My years spent with Daniel would certainly constitute emotional battering, but I grew accustomed to them, they became part of my daily existence. My body built up immunity to anything he threw at me—a zombie. Going through the motions.

But I couldn't rely on my emotions, erratic at the best of times lately. Would I ever be able to control them? I made a mental note to ask Belinda—she showed me what she could do, but it came naturally to her, no emotional involvement. Otherwise, the episode with the guards might've ended badly for them.

A knock at the door put my musings on hold. Moving would make my head explode and my stomach turn, so I shouted to whoever stood outside to let themselves in.

Even before I saw his face, every inch of my body tingled at Deacon's presence. My heart skipped a beat and my stomach flipped for all different reasons. If I tried to describe his beauty in words, I'd falter.

He took my breath away the moment his deep, dazzling eyes locked on mine. His gaze never wavered, even when he stepped over the threshold of my room and sauntered over to me in all his Godlike glory.

With his boyish smile, I forgot everything that plagued my mind. Butterflies danced their feverish beat in my stomach when he sat on the bed next to me. His fingers brushed mine and sent wave upon crashing wave of delicious heat through to my very soul.

"How are you feeling?" The sincere tone of his question posed several of my own.

Did he know?

Attempting a smile, I answered, "I'm OK, thank you."

"I've spoken to Lucas," *Bingo!* "He told me about your conversation."

I spent the next half hour explaining my feelings to Deacon and my concerns over Daniel. In turn, he told me what they dug up. He showed me a newspaper clipping describing the day of Daniel's father's death in detail. I felt sick, but I couldn't determine whether I felt pity for Daniel—for seeing his dad's death—or something entirely different.

Seeing his picture, a small, innocent boy, I wondered how he turned into such a monster. Regardless, he threatened me and my baby, so fear for our safety trumped all other emotions.

"There's something I need to ask you, Ellie."

He could ask me anything, especially if he continued to whisper my name the way he did. The moment it left his lips it floated through me like silk threads, and ignited lust-fuelled fires. A flame so intense, it surged through my body, sparking the irresistible urge to be consumed by him—something I craved the moment his eyes first met mine.

In a husky voice, laced with want, I asked, "What it is?"

"What was your mother's name?"

I wrinkled by brow. "My mum? Why do you need to know that?"

"So that we can be sure of your lineage."

Ah, made sense—witches were born of other witches, meaning my mum... *Jesus Christ,* did Dad know? I'd been only a few months old when Mum had died, Dad rarely talked about her death, it ate away at him—he loved her so much.

Deacon traced my cheek with his touch, delicate, gentle, wiping away a stray tear.

"Her name was Celeste." I adored her name, so beautiful—just like her.

Dad showed me pictures of her at my age. We shared the same chocolate waves and bright blue eyes. Her complexion flawless, skin like pure
porcelain and plump, bright red lips accentuated to the point of perfection...

"Oh my God!" I exclaimed. Deacon looked at me, eyebrows drawn. "The woman from my dreams is my mother."

∞∞∞

The shock realisation my mother visited me in my dreams confirmed my suspicions. *I am a witch.* No other explanation covered it—murder, magic, sacrifices, and ghosts of my past.

Wow. In all my twenty-one years, I would never have guessed my true identity. *I'm a Lancashire lass.* I worked in a pub to put myself through university, lived an average life with my dad, a few friends and an abusive boyfriend, whose child I now carried.

Now... *now I am something altogether different*, something—up until a decade ago—I only read about in books. *I'm a supernatural being,* in theory. So, by default, my child would be, too. I ran a hand over my belly and stared, bewildered, into the blue flames of the fire in the living quarters.

Deacon brought us here to talk to Lucas and Blake about my mother. Although, I figured they'd be able to tell me more than I could them.

My thoughts flickered back to Dad and whether or not he knew. I suspected not, otherwise he would have told me—he sucked at keeping secrets.

So, sat around the striking fire with three gorgeous vamps, I intended to listen while they told me I possessed magical powers.

I placed the newspaper clipping of Daniel's father's murder on the table surrounding the fire—I didn't know why I bought it along. I guess I didn't want it hanging around my personal space, too much of a reminder, and I did have questions of my own. But first, I needed to know what lay ahead for me and my child.

Putting my hands in my lap as I sat back—nerves rattled all to hell—I waited for someone to speak. Only, the lights went out and an almighty crash echoed through the building, causing violent tremors.

My stomach vaulted and I let out an astonished cry. I gripped onto Deacon like my life depended on it, afraid he'd move away and I'd lose him to the darkness.

The emergency lighting kicked it, a dim green hue reminding me of night vision goggles. I made out Deacon beside me—my arms still clutched his powerful, broad shoulders. Blake and Lucas moved around us.

Deacon glanced down at me, his purple eyes black in the weak lighting. He mouthed, *are you okay?* I nodded.

The silence turned ominous and my heart raced.

"Is everyone alright?" I recognised Lucas's voice.

"Head for the doors to the labs." Blake.

Deacon stood up beside me and took hold of my hand, lifting me to my feet. Leaving the recess of the seating area I stopped. This was no mere power cut as I had naively hoped. Rushed voices, several of them, filtered in from outside the main doors.

Deacon armed me back to the sofas before he made his way toward the noise.

My skin prickled—something didn't feel right. A chill rushed through my bones and I snapped my gaze to the entrance. I shouted at Deacon to move, but my feeble attempts were swallowed up by an almighty bang when the doors blasted open and smashed into the far wall.

My scream echoed over the sound of the explosion, and the fire now licking at the doorframe. Deacon lay about twenty feet away, a crumpled heap on the floor.

I screamed again—a shrill, stomach-churning sound that burned the back of my throat and left ringing in my ears. I panicked, made to run in Deacon's direction, but strong arms took hold of my weaker ones. Lucas on one side of me, Blake on the other, eyes dark and fangs down. They were squatted—poised for attack, hissing and growling like vicious animals towards the source of the commotion.

Is Deacon OK? I struggled in their tight grasp; I needed to get to him. *Please be okay.* I breathed an audible sigh of relief when I saw him stir. He shook his head and tried to get up, the explosion having disorientated him. When he collapsed to the floor again, I let out another head-splitting scream.

A bright, white light consumed my vision, briefly blinding me, and I realised my arms were free. I lurched toward Deacon, but a shape shot out from the side of my tunnel vision, and a strong hand gripped me tight around my throat.

A body-shaking pain shot through my neck and down my spine. I choked, grasping and scraping at the hand cutting off my air. Squeezing my eyes shut, I gasped in desperation, trying to block out the pain of my burning lungs.

My feet lifted off the ground and my eyes flew open. The look reflected back at me represented pure evil, eyes twitching at the corners, a hateful smile plastered across his shadowed features.

"Does someone have a soft spot for the blood sucker?" Daniel sneered at me.

I froze, solid with fear—I stopped writhing in his clutches, too stunned. Panic flooded my senses and bile rose up my throat. My body trembled. *How has he found me? How did he even get in?*

In the seconds that passed—though it seemed an eternity—Deacon lifted himself off the floor. A guttural growl escaped his throat.

"Let her go, Daniel," he snarled through clenched teeth.

Even above the fire roaring at the entrance, I could hear every angry breath Deacon took—slow and laboured, waiting for his moment.

"Well, well, Elora. You seem to have found yourself a dutiful pet."

Daniel turned and locked eyes with Deacon while he lowered me back to the floor—his grip loosened around my neck somewhat, enough for me to breathe a little at least. *Sweet, merciful Lord... air.*

"I won't ask again." Every word from Deacon's mouth sounded dangerously calm.

He edged forward and Lucas and Blake shifted behind me, their heavy breathing sounding close to my ears. Daniel tensed and his grip stiffened.

"Enough!" A female voice boomed, forceful and drawn out. It filled my body with icy dread.

I hummed with the power emanating from her black soul.

I sensed at least one other person besides her, but she held more influence.

Closing my eyes tight, I channelled everything I could into homing in on the two newcomers. I focused so hard, until all other sensations dispersed—the pain in my neck, the raging fire, the thump of heartbeats and the heavy breathing of the General and his warriors.

Forgetting my place, I tried to gauge an understanding of the enemy. One stood out to me, but I didn't know why. I could almost hear her thoughts when I concentrated hard enough. Nothing intelligible, though—evil laughter, blood-curdling screams, venomous curses... *Holy Hell...* hate, death, blood, so much blood, and darkness—an infinite darkness. Pure loathing and degraded thoughts moulded together to form a sour, acidic taste in my mouth.

Jacob's frantic, hurried voice filtered through one of the closed doors and my focus waned. He'd heard the explosion, knew of the danger, could probably smell it.

A baby's cry echoed from somewhere deep within the building—followed by a shrill, ear-piercing screech, shattering what remained of the glass in the burning doorframe.

One of the strangers bolted toward the sound. She didn't get very far before Blake appeared in front of her. Chest puffed out, he forced his arms forward and smashed the witch in the chest. She flew back.

Landing against the wall with a sickening thud, she raised her head in time to see Blake in hot pursuit. I registered surprise when, whatever speed she lacked when making her dash forward, she more than made up for when she yanked a wooden stake from the long cloak concealing her face and body. Despite the fact that she must be winded, she launched her weapon at Blake. Muttering something incoherent, the large spike burned gold for a brief second.

I couldn't tear my gaze away from the scene unfolding. The stake flew through the air, its aim true. Blake tilted his body at the last minute in an obvious effort to deflect the weapon.

The missile embedded itself in his shoulder, a twelve inch bullet the unnatural force of which catapulted him back into the wall, impaling him.

He didn't yell out, but his face contorted in pain and fury while he flailed about, trying to prise the stake from his shoulder.

Hours seemed to pass, but in reality barely a minute.

The doors behind me crashed and splintered amid Jacob's deafening battle cry—all too late. The presence I recognised earlier made herself known.

Ember.

She darted so fast from the shadows and headed straight for the source of the noise. I twisted to see Jacob's bulging eyes register his shock. Lucas moved to help him.

Did Ember really think she could take on two vampires, centuries older than her?

It made no difference, I realised all too late the intended distraction. Daniel reached for something inside his coat—a small vial of murky liquid.

Without another word, Daniel threw the concoction to the ground—three more shattered around me—and a choking, thick mist erupted. It shot up and licked at the ceiling with animated tentacles. They snaked out in all directions, long wispy arms seeking to cover every possible inch of space.

The cloying substance made me sick and dizzy. My head spun and my eyes rolled backward. Muffled, desperate voices called my name. I lost all feeling in my body before darkness hauled me asunder.

∞ ∞ ∞

The room filled with a thick, black smog enveloping everybody in it—heads became fuzzy, movements sluggish, like the space between reality and dreaming.

Deacon snapped out of his haze when the frame of the entryway collapsed into a smouldering heap on the floor. Taking in his surroundings—dim light, fire, his brothers on their hands and knees—something seemed... off.

He put a hand to his pounding head—he felt drunk. *What the hell just happened?*

A soft groan disturbed his train of thought.

Blake. Half pinned to a wall, a stake protruded from his shoulder. Lucas and Jacob were slumped on the floor, stunned and confused.

Deacon steeled a glance in other directions, something still amiss. Wishing his head would clear so he could think straight, he stood, off-balance, and looked from Blake to Jacob to Lucas, his brow creasing.

Elora!

He let out a sharp growl and bounded for the door.

"Wait!" Lucas may well have been dazed, but his voice still held a commanding edge.

Deacon slowed, trying to figure out why his General would stop him pursuing the enemy—an enemy with *his* Elora in their clutches. Rage bubbled inside him and he suppressed a growl as he spun to face his leader.

He settled his focus on Lucas. "What are we waiting for? They have Ellie. They're going to kill her." His fangs were still in place and a red hue clouded his vision.

"She's safe, for the time being," Lucas told him.

Deacon panted through gritted teeth, "What do you mean, she's safe?"

Lucas explained, while Deacon spoke with Elora, he busied himself scrutinising everything Belinda told them. She stated she knew how the victims were being selected—everyone assumed because of their infertility, their need for a child. Lucas suspected something else, so re-questioned Belinda only to discover the victims were selected in accordance with their birth sign.

Witches drew their power from the sign under which they were born. Morgan drew hers from the earth, Gillian fire, Ivy air and Belinda water. Cassandra still needed a water sign because Belinda escaped. While Lucas spoke with her, she went into labour, both mother and child now secure in the medical ward.

"What sign is Elora?" Deacon asked, exasperated.

"She's fire; born August tenth."

"I don't get it." Deacon shook his head in confusion. "Why has she been taken, then?"

"Elora is to be the fifth sacrifice, and it has something to do with her mother."

Deacon stood rigid. "Do you know who her mother is?"

"Not entirely, but we need to find out."

"We don't have time to find out. They aren't going to sit around and wait for us to deliver Belinda to them. They will find someone else and then they will kill Ellie."

Deacon's emotions spiked to dangerous levels. Consumed by the need to save his mate—the single most important thing to him—he would not let her die, he couldn't live without her. They needed one another, now more than ever.

"They have her in their clutches. They may not kill her just yet, but they can certainly do other things to her. How the fuck does that make her safe?" Deacon fumed, his voice bellowing out above all else.

"Deacon, you will watch your tongue with me," Lucas started. "I understand your turmoil, but rushing in blind will get both you and Elora killed."

A commotion from outside the room startled them. They braced themselves, assuming a second attack.

"What the hell happened here?" Chloe came into view, paving a careful way around the burning debris.

Deacon's body relaxed when he saw her walk through the door, a young woman in tow.

Lucas shifted to stand beside him, asking, "Is this Madison Rose?"

"Yes," the young woman replied in a meek voice, observing the devastation around her.

"You have something to show us?" Deacon all but growled, hasty in his hope to find out if whatever she possessed could help save Elora.

"I do."

Lucas turned on his heel and beckoned everyone to follow. Without glancing back, he pointed in Blake's direction, "Get him off the wall, then bring everyone to the labs."

Deacon looked over at Blake, still struggling to free himself. Under any other circumstances, Deacon would have found the sight hilarious, but right now he could see nothing but blood red fury.

Every inch of his aching soul screamed at him to run after Elora, he fought against it with all the control he could muster. It tugged at his heart. He could *feel* her anguish, and everywhere he looked, he saw her pained face.

She is meant for me, and I for her. I will tear every psychotic, demon cock-sucking bitch apart until she is safe in my arms again. His whole body itched to turn and bolt for the door, but the same burning love he felt for her held him back. He agreed with Lucas—if he went in blind, they'd both end up dead.

∞∞∞

What on earth is Ember doing working with witches? No doubt, a question on everyone's mind while they made their way to the labs.

Lucas pondered over why her General let her live for her earlier indiscretion. Deacon screamed that he wanted to rip the bitch's head off, and Blake informed everyone he recognised her scent from Belinda's house, not to mention her speed—unnaturally fast, even for a vampire.

Nate and Sam were caught up to speed when they arrived back a little after Chloe.

Once downstairs, Lucas set up the projection unit for the video Madison captured.

The witch explained how Ivy had sent her away from the house the moment a car pulled up outside the gates, but she couldn't do it. Fear and guilt kept her hidden in the surrounding woods while she watched two people enter her home.

Through the upstairs window—the altar room—Madison watched candlelight flicker off the walls before the majority were snuffed out. An unnerving silence sent her running back to the house. She peered through the kitchen window while she fumbled with her phone, intent on calling the police, but movement and hushed voices made her switch to her camera.

Lucas played the recording.

The footage showed the Swanson's empty kitchen, but the dim sound of the video produced muffled voices, movements growing louder before two women entered the room. The faded lighting left much to be desired, but the Faction's heightened vision enabled them to make out a tall, skinny woman with long, black hair and an exotic complexion.

The raven-haired beauty's lean form moved to shield the other witch from view, but not before the team caught a glimpse of the bundle she carried. The phone's microphone picked up Madison's stifled cry when the bundle moved and gurgled.

The kitchen disappeared from view—Madison explained she ducked low to avoid detection. Seconds later it came back. Both women headed for the door leading outside. The tall lady went first, leaving an unobstructed view of the witch carrying the child. Everyone stared at the screen with varying expressions, most having no clue who they were looking at.

Sam found his voice first, "Son of a bitch, that's Darcy."

Chapter 17

I came to in a large, lavish living room, on an Edwardian chaise longue. A huge stone fireplace stood in front of me, Daniel leaned against it talking to some voluptuous blonde piece and fingering her hair.

Nausea clawed up my throat, but I shook it off and swallowed hard. My head swam, dense, as though someone had sat on it for a couple of hours. I stood on leaden legs and stared at Daniel, my mind willing him to spontaneously combust in front of me in writhing, excruciating agony. He stole his gaze away from the blonde long enough to notice my movements. Strolling toward me, his lips curled into a sneer.

I froze—my brain shut down—I wanted to move out the way of Daniel and whatever vicious punishment his grimacing face told me he wanted to reign down on me. His evil, squinted eyes sent icy chills racing down my spine and a cold sweat broke on my forehead. My heart raced, palms sweated. I balled and un-balled my fists, attempting to make my feet edge backwards, but they wouldn't budge, my legs too heavy.

Stood tall in front of me, he swiped the back of his hand across my face. I turned and landed awkwardly on the chaise.

"Be careful, you damn fool. The baby." A female voice bellowed behind me.

Through the sting to my face, a surge of energy started at the bottom of my legs—like pins and needles, but stronger, faster—shooting its heated way up my thighs, through my stomach, and down my arms to my hand. Every nerve ending in my body tingled.

I flung my hand out when Daniel reached me. It didn't make contact with him, but a burst of sparks from my fingertips sent him careening across the room and into the blonde, causing a pained scream to tear through her.

I stared at the unfolding scene. *Unbelievable,* although, it shouldn't have been, not really, not anymore.

Daniel teetered on the verge of consciousness, but shook himself off and slumped against the wall. He looked right into my eyes, bemused, but also a little scared, his face pale, eyes searching. I glanced down at my outstretched hand, turning it back and forth.

I still stared at it when pain exploded across my face for the second time, coursing down my neck and spine. It took a moment to register the blonde in front of me—my mind still unravelling what just happened—her arm still raised from the slap she gave me.

Glaring at her, I clutched my face and lifted my other hand, I stopped short of smacking the bitch back when that voice sounded from behind me again. Calmer this time.

"I wouldn't do that, if I were you. Keira has a nasty temper on her, and I can't afford for you to die just yet."

Spinning around, I locked eyes with a tall, skinny woman, jet black hair bundled in a messy pile atop her head. She dressed in a thin piece of black cloth, constituting a dress of sorts that reached the floor and pooled at her feet. A slash to the thigh exposed smooth, olive skin, but the plunging neckline did nothing for her flat chest.

Her dark eyes bore into mine, making my skin prickle when her face broke into an unnerving, cruel smile. I tried to swallow, but my throat turned bone dry. She radiated darkness and I wanted to cower under her glare.

Two women entered behind the lean, waif-like thing. One around my height—about five foot four—with short, brown hair and a curvy figure spilling out of the purple laced corset she wore.

The other, another frail looking atrocity with a pale, gaunt face emphasised by baby pink hair—*that has to be a wig.*

"Cassandra, it's time," Pink Wig addressed the exotic woman.

Cassandra! *Daniel is involved. And I am a target.*

I swayed on my feet, dizziness and nausea battled together, forcing me to sit down on the sofa again. *Why? How?* I'd been such a fool—trying to please him, to make things work between us. I didn't want to fail and all this time the son of a bitch played me! Did he know of my past, my lineage? How, when I had no clue? There were so many questions in need of answers before my sanity well and truly left the building.

In my shell-shocked state, I threw Cassandra a passing glance, she nodded to the two women and they left the room, only to reappear moments later dragging a pregnant, light-haired woman with them.

The restrained woman kicked and screamed, cried until she choked. My senses picked up on her fear. It poured from her very core while Little and Large marched her toward the far wall.

Cassandra closed her eyes and chanted, arms half raised. I smelled burning. Wisps of smoke plumed from the floor behind the sofa in front of me. The witch's eyes snapped open and inky, black pools shone back at me.

In a swift movement, the scared woman's body catapulted against the wall with a bone-crunching thud, an agonised yelp escaped her lips. The smoke dancing at Cassandra's feet began to swirl around the stricken woman, curling around her wrists and ankles. She began to thrash about, screaming stomach-turning sounds I'd never forget, but the smoke held her in place.

While Cassandra concentrated, the top heavy witch moved to stand in front of the panicked girl. The imprisoned woman's screams grew louder when the sadistic bitch pulled out a familiar knife.

Bile raked its way up my throat. The mad witch raised the blade and I lurched forward instinctively, screaming.

Two hands grabbed hold of my arms from behind in a rough, calloused grip. But the moment the knife plunged into the pregnant woman's chest, my legs gave out and I collapsed.

I tried so hard to tear my gaze away, but the same hands restraining me held my jaw firm, forced me to watch while the lunatic witch gutted her victim. Blood pumped out, spurting over the psycho and coating the surrounding area in thick, crimson splashes. The sound made my stomach turn, the tearing, slicing, squelching. I heaved.

When the witch pulled the dead woman's child from her stomach I emptied the contents of mine onto the floor.

The hands around my face loosened and I grabbed hold of the sofa to haul myself up. On shaky legs I stood, squaring my shoulders and raising my chin to stare at the horror before me. Chest heaving, I attempted to put one foot in front of the other. *I need to get out of here; my baby will not die in this place.*

"Where do you think you're going, sweetheart?" Daniel asked from behind me, his tone sarcastic and condescending. "I told you I'd make you pay, bitch."

I turned and spat back, "Fuck you." I didn't have any other plausible answer to his question, but I felt the need to say something in retaliation.

He put his hands on his hips, a conceited, mocking smile played on his face before he laughed at me again. I *hated* that sound, I hated him—I hated him with a passion I couldn't describe—I wanted to see him die a painful, bloody death.

I wanted to be the one to put an end to him, to gut him throat to groin, witness the life ebb from *his* body and rejoice in it.

He would *not* get his demonic hands on my child. None of them would.

Rage burned through me, my body heated and prickled. I panted, heavy and rasping. I advanced on him, the smile falling from his face, but from the corner of my eye I saw Cassandra turn to face me. Affording her a glance, I noted her trembling limbs and paling complexion, her eyes still two ebony orbs of nothingness.

She pushed her hands out and the black, misty tendrils holding the dead woman to the wall raced toward me.

I stilled, tilting my head, still consumed and locked by my hate for Daniel and thoughts of how I wanted him to suffer.

The black fog circled my body, warm, but uncomfortable. My skin heated, burning almost—like sitting out in the blazing sun, coated in oil. My mind clouded over, vision faded in and out, yet oddly my brain kept questioning, before the darkness claimed me, why the woman against the wall remained there unaided.

∞∞∞

Amelia struggled to open her eyes as roaring pain thumped through her head. A drying substance cracked down her face when she grimaced.

Attempting to rub her temples, a clanging sound rang out and a sharp pain lanced through her arm. Prising her eyes open, she turned her head, ignoring the agony shooting down her neck. With groggy recognition, she noticed rusted, metal shackles restraining her wrists, her ankles, too.

Turning her attention forward, she squeezed her eyes together, blinking hard a couple of times to remove the white stars dancing in her vision.

Through the dim light she tried to make sense of her surroundings—alone in a small, bare-bricked cell with no windows, but a large wooden door housing a small, barred outlet near the top. The room smelled like damp and neglect on top of death and decay. The pungent stench clawed at the back of Amelia's throat like a thick, viscous liquid.

Disembodied voices floated down outside the door. Amelia looked out the window; the dense darkness disturbed by the odd, intermittent flicker of an orange glow... a flame, perhaps?

The whole scene possessed a 'medieval dungeon' atmosphere, and Amelia half expected an executioner in a black hooded mask to come for her and cut her head off with a rusted axe. She shuddered at the thought.

Lifting her head, she examined the shackles again—*Jesus, they really do belong in some fifteenth century torture chamber*—seeing thick, heavy chains connected to the chunky, metal cuffs. *Well, they won't be breaking any time soon*; she tugged on them a few times to prove the point.

The clanging reverberated around the tiny room—too loud for the eerily quiet atmosphere—and she cringed at the echo bouncing off the walls outside the cell.

The chatter stopped, replaced by hurried footsteps making their way closer. Through the vague lighting, Amelia saw a pair of eyes peering at her through the bars of her cell door, the expression scrunched into a smile.

"She's awake," they called out in a honeyed tone.

The eyes disappeared, replaced by the rattle of keys before the call door opened with a resounding creak and a tall, lean woman stepped into the room—ducking down to accommodate her height.

"Inspector Ellis, I'm glad you could finally join us."

How does she know my name? Amelia wondered.

"My name is Cassandra." Her mocking smile made ghastly from the shadows in the cell. "You can call me Sister Hewitt, or Priestess."

"I'd rather not, if it's all the same. What do you want with me, and what have you done with Darcy?"

"Oh yes, Darcy. We know her here as Sister Simms."

Amelia's brow furrowed at Cassandra's choice of words when Darcy walked into the room, amusement sparkling in her viridian-green eyes.

"What the hell is going on here?" Amelia shouted, panicked.

"Well, I would've thought it was plainly obvious, Inspector. You've been duped." Cassandra's aristocratic voice grated on her.

Amelia's bewildered gaze went from the Priestess to her colleague. "Darcy... ?"

"That's right, Amelia. I'm a witch, and I was right under your nose this whole time." Darcy laughed a sickening, evil sound.

Amelia clamped her mouth shut, teeth gritted together—words failed her. She felt anger, rage in fact, but couldn't string together a coherent sentence. Her own constable, someone she thought highly of and demonstrated such passion for the job, practiced the occult, and took part in the ritualistic sacrifice of innocent women and children.

"But... why? The babies--?

Darcy threw her head back and laughed again. Amelia's anger ramped up several notches.

"I've been a witch all of my life, Amelia. The Priestess taught my mother. This is my calling. To raise Lilith and serve her purpose."

Amelia sneered, "What purpose?"

"The purpose she was always meant to have. To rule the world with men beneath her, where they belong. To raise an army of strong, fierce women to stand beside her."

Amelia laughed—she couldn't help it, it sounded ridiculous. "Are you fuckin' crazy, you psychotic bitch? Have you heard yourself?"

Her laughter rang through the cell, cut short when Darcy marched over to her and slapped her hard, in the face. Amelia tasted blood, but couldn't hold back her smirk as she spat mucus-y, red fluid onto the floor.

"You really are deranged, aren't you? You wait until I'm outta here, you sick fuck. I'll hunt you down and gut you like you did those poor women. I'll make sure you die in pain." She clenched her teeth and spat the words in Darcy's face.

Darcy and Cassandra laughed a disgusting, depraved sound. They walked out of the cell, the door slamming shut behind them. The lock clicked into place. Laughter resonated down the corridor and Amelia hung her head.

Chapter 18

Amid his own fretful strides, Deacon watched Blake pace the Compound's living area, angst spread across his stricken face. Since learning of Amelia's trip to Simonstone with Darcy, the team tried countless times to get hold of her on her mobile, but with no luck. Blake complained of a sick, uneasy tension burrowing in the pit of his stomach.

The older vampire's own body shook, the blood thirsty monster buried deep within bursting at the seams to get out, to cause pain and destruction to anyone who dared get in its way. The colossal effort to keep it at bay weighed on him. His face screwed up in torture, fists balled by his sides, his stride angry and resolute while he pictured Elora's face in the moments of her capture.

Sam and Chloe kept quiet, a testament to their shock upon learning one of their own played a part in these hideous murders. In particular, Chloe recounted her emotions upon seeing the gruesome devastation—disgust, horror. She questioned over and over how someone they knew, a friend no less, could be involved in such atrocities? Sam looked void of all feeling. He sat, head in hands and stared at nothing, waiting while time ticked by.

Nate and Madison occupied one of the computers. Madison recognised Celeste's name—her own grandmother, Rhea, had been taught by her many years ago, passing on her teachings to the motherless sisters.

Rhea also taught them about a different kind of witch—a Superior Priestess—a witch of such supreme power, able to control all the elements, in tune with all of nature being able to hone her senses in on anything she wanted. The Superior Priestess could talk to animals, read from wildlife and feel the emotions of the earth.

The level of control required for such power must be taught. Celeste had been a Superior Priestess and with her death, Elora inherited the power. But her death also meant Elora never learned how to use it, never even knew of her gifts. Her magic lay dormant in her until her twenty-first birthday—a witch's coming of age—where her powers sprouted unaided. With the lack of guidance and knowledge, the magic inside her now presented itself, uncontrolled and possibly dangerous in her struggle to maintain it.

In the meantime, Lucas—glued to another laptop—looked for anything that might give them an advantage. The team shared the notion that the witches would be certain they knew their location since taking Amelia, so using the element of surprise did not seem such a plausible idea.

They needed a way to get into the house undetected, so Lucas searched for the blueprints in the hopes they would show him some other way in. Only when Madison revealed what she knew about the place did Lucas start to divulge his plan.

"There's an underground tunnel leading into the basement of the house," she offered.

"How do you know this?" Lucas' face lit up and he held his breath.

"My sister told me. One of the witches liked to run her mouth when she was drunk or high, and she spilled the beans about it. Ivy told me because she always felt uneasy being in that house; she needed an escape route in case things turned... ." She trailed off and choked back tears.

Chloe put her arm around Madison's shoulders and whispered gentle words of comfort to her.

Once she composed herself, Madison showed Lucas the location of the tunnel and he devised their plan of attack before sending Nate away to get additional help.

∞∞∞

Amelia—past caring who heard her—rattled the chains in the vain hope she might find a reserve of super human strength to yank them from the wall. No such luck.

She refused to die down here, but she began to lose faith until a moment of sudden realisation slapped her like a cold cloth around the face.

She strove to reach her head, the chains were long enough, but the cuffs dug into her wrists. She fumbled with her hair, grunting with the effort, and smiled when she pulled one of the grips free.

A flutter coasted through her stomach followed by a surge of hope. *Now if only I can master lock-picking,* she stretched one arm over to fiddle with the lock on the cuff.

Not daring to blink during the struggle to free herself, her eyes strained from the effort. Sweat beaded her forehead, but she let out a half-breath when a clink indicated of one of her shackles had popped open. It hit the wall with a clang and she stilled, listening for any sign of movement outside.

Interminable moments passed before she resumed her attempt at undoing the other handcuff—satisfied no-one made their way to inspect the noise. Her whole body trembled, perspiration seeped from every possible place. Her mouth went bone dry while she held her breath again.

Amelia succeeded in popping all the restraints, but stopped when she heard footsteps hurrying down the corridor. Panic rising, she fought the urge to hyperventilate, racking her brains for what she could do next.

Sidling against the wall next to the door, she thought, *really?* Whoever looked in would be able to see she managed to free herself.

Think, Amelia, think, she willed herself. Amelia whipped off her blazer and held it over the window. Not convinced it would work, but willing to try anything, she prayed her desperation would pay off.

Her breath caught in her throat when the footsteps stopped outside the door. She listened, trying to gauge the reaction of whoever stood outside. The clatter of keys rang out again—the movements frantic. *Is this actually working?!* She'd laugh at the fool under any other circumstances.

The lock snapped and Amelia pulled her blazer from over the window. The door opened. Amelia yanked it further, grabbed the stranger by the hair and slammed their head into a wall. A sickening crunch of bone against brick resonated around the small chamber.

Amelia dragged the immobile figure further into the cell, shutting the door behind her. She glanced down at the unmoving form of Darcy, unconscious at her feet. Blood seeped down her forehead.

Searching for the keys, Amelia realise they must've fallen outside of the door. She shuffled over and stood by it, listening for any sounds. Certain no-one waited outside, she gently pried the door open, wincing when it creaked, holding her breath—again.

Bending down, she snatched the set of three rusted keys from the corridor floor and closed the door behind her a touch faster, to lessen the risk of it groaning.

Finally free, she needed to find a way out of this primitive prison unseen.

∞ ∞ ∞

With each second that ticked by, each time they went over and over the plan, Deacon became more impatient, aggravated and panicked. *What the fuck is taking so damn long?* He pictured Elora's beautiful face and tried not to imagine the consequences of them being too late to save her with all this redundant, repetitive babble.

He paced the floor. Back and forth, back and forth, stopping only to give his input where he thought it necessary, striving to keep the beast within contained.

His anxious thoughts were cut short when Bernie came running into the room, dread etched across his features, eyes wide searching the room for him.

"Where is she? Please tell me she's OK." He grabbed Deacon by his powerful arms and drew on a strength belying his stature, while he shook Deacon for all his worth.

"Calm down, B. We know where she is. We'll find her."

Bernie turned to Lucas as he spoke, but he didn't relinquish his hold on Deacon. The younger vampire started to feel the pinch from Bernie's tightening grasp.

Bernie looked a pale, frightened mess—understandably. But he calmed himself and loosened his vice-like grip on Deacon. Lucas approached and placed a reassuring hand on his trembling shoulder.

"We're going for her now, B. I promise we'll bring her back safe."

Lucas did not break his promises easily, but then again, the threat lying before them remained unknown. Deacon prayed his General would be able to keep his word. And not just for Bernie.

Lucas turned to Deacon. "You ready for this big guy? I need you level headed."

Deacon raised his rigid chin, stared into his boss's eyes and nodded once. He couldn't afford to fail, not with Elora's life at stake.

Lucas turned back to the group. "Get your gear together, we leave in five."

∞∞∞

Amelia tried hard to keep her body from trembling, but it proved difficult—she witnessed first-hand what those lunatics were capable of. If she thought she knew fear before, it didn't hold a candle to this. A gun held to her head? No comparison. Facing off against a gang of youths armed with broken bottles and knives? No comparison.

All of her past experiences did not compare to the thought of someone ripping her stomach open while conscious, and being held down by a demon burning a hole through her flesh. Not being with child made it *less* likely to happen, but not any less terrifying that something still *could*.

In the minutes that passed, Amelia locked Darcy in the cell, stuffing the Constable's police-issue neckerchief into her mouth. Though, Darcy would need to break out of the shackles first. Amelia wouldn't allow the traitorous bitch any opportunity to alert someone.

The corridor felt stifling, or perhaps Amelia's nerves were getting the better of her. She started to feel claustrophobic until she noticed a door just ahead of her—sturdy oak and studded. *Right out of some long forgotten castle.* This one contained no window to peer in or out, so Amelia swallowed hard and edged her way closer.

Putting her ear to the door, she listened, but couldn't hear a damn thing. Whether the thickness of the door impeded her hearing, or no-one actually stood on the other side of it, she couldn't be sure. One thing felt certain, though, she did not revel in the sinking feeling swirling in her gut.

After a couple of deep breaths, she tried the handle. *Locked.* She slipped one of the keys into the lock, twisting it. *Bingo! First time lucky,* she rejoiced.

Amelia braced herself against the clicking of the lock, expecting it to sound forty times louder than it did. Relief swam through her when she barely noticed it. The creak of the door opening, however, sent her thundering heart on a one-way attempt through her chest—and not for the first time today.

Amelia cringed, going from heated cheeks and dripping sweat to ice cold and ready to faint. Her eyes remained fixed on the door, alert. Counting the seconds against the thumping of her heart, she breathed a heavy sigh of relief when nothing happened. Slowly, she poked her head out the door.

No-one came at her, so she stepped out of the corridor and into a large hallway with an attached dining room. Darkness permeated the area in a gloomy blanket. The only light came from a few, dim wall lamps, but the entire area yielded an eerie, unsettling aura.

Amelia expected to see a headless ghost float toward her from some darkened corner of the house. She thanked God it didn't happen—her quaking nerves wouldn't have allowed for her to handle it very well.

Adjusting to the lack of light, she noted the dining room housed several huge windows, curtains drawn back. Thick, dark clouds allowed a miniscule amount of moonlight to filter through, only to be eaten up by the black veil shrouding the house.

The hallway to Amelia's right reminded her of an old game show. A group of kids would lead another wearing a sight-impairing helmet around medieval dungeons and such like, fighting all kinds of beasts and monsters. Amelia mimicked that blind kid, but with no-one to lead her to safety, she needed to find her own way out. She prayed her escape didn't involve battling fantastical creatures.

Unable to pick out any escape route in the hallway—the walls covered floor to ceiling in big, heavy curtains—Amelia headed toward the dining room. The partial lighting shed on it also meant less chance of any spooks or spectres getting the jump on her in the darkness… or so she told herself.

Weaponless—having been stripped of her possessions during her comatose state—and airing on the side of fear, she tiptoed around the solid oak table. Amelia found it odd she couldn't hear anything. Perhaps the witches were upstairs. If so, they could bloody well stay there while she looked for a way out down here.

She edged her way around the wall of the hallway-cum-dining area and came to a large oak, double door. It looked thick and heavy and she grew a little concerned it might make a delightful creaking noise like the one to the basement.

An eternity seemed to pass while Amelia stood loitering outside the large doors—she figured she didn't really want to see what lay on the other side in case someone heard her and waited for her entrance.

Instead, she made her way over to the huge windows, peering out across the bleak, rain-swept countryside. Storm clouds amalgamated into one big, grey mass leaving a dark, foreboding atmosphere hanging over the house. Rain came down in thunderous torrents, lashing off the windows and bouncing off the gravel drive.

Searching the frames, Amelia couldn't see any handles until she came to the middle of the three sets. Large, black metal catches were set some distance above Amelia's head. She reached up and grabbed a firm grip on one. She tried to force it either side, but it wouldn't budge. Amelia's heart sank.

"Shit!" she hissed through gritted teeth.

Making her way back to the wooden door, she placed an ear on the surface, listening for any noises on the other side. But like the basement door, the thickness could easily be obstructing her hearing—nothing floated through.

Letting out a long breath, Amelia squared her shoulders and cricked her neck—*now or never,* she thought. Attempting to swallow past her cotton-dry throat, she reached for the door knob, suppressing the choke trying to claw its way up. Sick with nerves, she twisted the handle and the door swung inward.

She stepped foot into a large room—at least thirty square meters—with a stone flagged floor and similar lattice windows to the ones in the dining room, equal in size. A huge, bricked fireplace accommodated one wall with an oil painting of some hellish landscape above it.

The rest of the room scream tasteful décor—reds and golds with expensive period furniture, rugs and drapery. A quick glance to her far right highlighted a set of patio doors leading outside. She moved toward them, but something to the left caught her eye.

Slick blood trailed in thick smears down the wall, creating a large void. The crimson ooze pooled on the luxurious carpet and formed a coagulated puddle of deep red. An unexpected shudder ran through Amelia's body.

Striding toward the patio doors, she passed a small telephone table and noted a stack of paperwork spilling out the drawer—junk mail, solicitor letters, insurance documents. Somehow, Amelia couldn't associate that barbaric murderess with this kind of everyday normalcy. About to walk straight past, she stopped to look at something that caught her attention.

Contemplating the evidence in front of her, she jumped when a pained scream rang through her ears. A body rushed her, rugby tackling her to the ground. The two slid through the gelatinous blood on the floor.

Amelia grabbed hold of her attacker's arms and threw her aside. The weight of the body caused the sofa to shift forward as it careened into the back of it.

"You bitch!" Darcy stood and shook herself off while Amelia lay on her back in the crimson puddle.

The constable advanced, dark blood still oozing down the side of her face, eyes wide and wild while Amelia backed away. The crazed maniac launched a booted foot at Amelia's stomach, causing her to wail and clutch her belly. A slap to Amelia's face followed, before the DCI grabbed hold of Darcy's ankle and yanked her leg from under her.

The witch fell backward and cracked her head against the sofa. Amelia used Darcy's dazed state to her advantage and jumped to her feet. Before the Constable could right herself, Amelia smashed her fist into the side of Darcy's face, almost joining her on the floor, but regained her balance.

Darcy howled an unnatural sound and scrambled forward. Amelia used the moment to look for a defensive weapon, noting the old-fashioned, iron poker by the fireplace. She ran for it, but Darcy tackled her and the two of them crashed through the mahogany table in the centre of the room.

Amelia rolled on to her front to get up, but Darcy grabbed the back of her head and attempted to pummel it off the floor beneath them. Amelia pushed against the floor with the flat of her hands, using the leverage to turn herself over. The effort afforded her another slap to the face before Darcy straddled her and tightened two hands around her neck, squeezing with a strength defying her stature.

Amelia's lungs burned and white dots danced around her vision. She grappled around the floor above her head, searching for something she could use to force Darcy away from her.

Her hand fingered something solid and hard and she grasped at it before launching it at Darcy's head.

The sharp end of the splintered table leg penetrated Darcy's neck with a sickening squelch. Her eyes bulged and thick globules of crimson dribbled from the corners of her lips and down her chin. The witch coughed and warm blood splattered Amelia's face and neck before she pushed Darcy off her, groaning over killing a woman she once considered a friend.

Lindsey Jayne

She shook herself out of her torn, bloodied jacket, breathing hard, while she stared at Darcy's innate body.

Chapter 19

Deacon shifted in his seat. His body shook, and he clenched and unclenched his fists under the increasing tension. The drive to Cassandra's Simonstone mansion seemed to take an age—he opted to ride with Chloe in her car. He didn't trust himself to give the roads his full attention on his bike. Blake also rode in one of the cars from the Compound, Madison driving, after she refused to be left behind in an already breached building. Lucas and Sam screamed ahead on their bikes.

The monster inside Deacon itched to spring free, but he needed to remain level-headed for everyone's sake, especially Elora's. Losing his humanity could put her in harm's way, but if any one of those witches already drew even a pinprick of her blood, he would not be able to quell the beast. It would destroy anything in its path.

Lost in thought, he failed to notice Chloe pulling up near Cassandra's. Lucas stood waiting, an imposing figure in the dreary atmosphere. Sam, Blake and Madison pulled up moments later.

Everyone congregated at the gates to the property.

"Madison, Chloe, Sam, you've studied the blueprints, you know where to go?" Lucas asked them in turn, wasting no time.

Madison nodded before she beckoned Sam and Chloe to follow her. The three of them ran into the dense woodland surrounding Cassandra's home.

Lucas nodded at Deacon and Blake. The three of them then leapt with lithely silence over the front gates, and disappeared into the murky depths of the trees lining the long driveway.

*

Madison, Sam and Chloe wound their way through heavy woodland to get to their destination. Nothing much in the way of light penetrated the thick canopy of trees overhead. Chloe wished she'd bought her torch with her—the three of them used the backlights from their mobile phones to find their way.

Madison warned the two officers that the basement they were headed for would not turn out to be the large wine cellar the plans depicted it to be—Cassandra turned it into a dungeon of sorts.

When Ivy became increasingly afraid of Cassandra and her little group of reprobates, she advised Madison of the cellar's location—an escape route, should she need it.

So far as Madison knew, Cassandra didn't possess knowledge of the secret tunnel's location; it didn't show up on any development plans. Nevertheless, she took precaution by enchanting the entrance.

The witch explained, for Chloe's curiosity, that aside from drawing power from their birth sign, a white witch could cast simple protection spells or illusions, providing they didn't directly harm another person.

"So, black witches are different?" Chloe asked.

Madison nodded. She clarified that black witches, or at least the High Priestess of a black coven, were once white witches. The magic they possessed was never enough for them—they thrived on power and the more they possessed, the more corrupt they became because of it. In the end, their selfish desires and acts consumed them until their souls and hearts turned jet black.

Unfortunately, a black witch's power could not be limited to one element of nature, because nature refused to acknowledge their evil alignment. They drew on the unlimited powers of Hell to cause whatever devastation they wished, because Hell held no qualms with death and destruction, nor power and greed.

They still needed teaching, though, and a High Priestess would take on witches beneath her, with similar dark intentions, to coach them in the use of their catastrophic magic.

Madison's explanation ended when they reached their location. Rummaging through the overgrowth of foliage, she uncovered a slim, wooden door set in the ground.

"It's padlocked and chained." Chloe looked over the witch's shoulder.

Madison nodded. "I put them there."

Sam walked up to the trapdoor and examined the padlock in his hand, his brow creasing. "There's no keyhole."

Madison giggled at his naivety. "Of all the things you've likely seen, and still you don't have a clue." She brushed past him, waving her hand over the padlock. It snapped open.

"Cool." Sam drew out the word in a childlike manner. A big grin erupted on his face—he looked like someone who'd never clapped eyes on a naked lady before, and had been handed a load of porn mags.

"Bless your innocence, Samuel."

He cast Chloe a sideways squint and she chuckled at him, knowing he hated his full name.

Madison removed the chains and threw back the doors to reveal a dark, dank stone staircase. She made her way down.

"Come on, dumbass." Chloe clipped Sam around the head and beckoned for him to follow her and Madison into the pitch black tunnel.

The shaft seemed a whole lot longer given that the only light source still came from three mobile phones. Madison led the way, groping along the slimy, moss coated walls. The whole passageway smelt like damp and something else no one could quite put their finger on. Something macabre.

The uneven, slippery floor made progress slow—on more than one occasion each of them needed to cling to the wall, or one another to stop from falling flat on their arses.

They stayed silent, too scared of the unknown, the unseen, but most of all for what they might unwittingly walk into when they found their way out of this God forsaken rabbit hole.

Madison stifled a cry of relief when they reached the end of the tunnel. She noted the rusted rungs of an old ladder leading up to an aged grate in the ceiling.

"I can move the grate, but I can't stop the noise at the same time. Someone needs to go up there and move it while I silence the area."

Sam went up and inspected the treads in the wall—they looked old and corroded—they felt a tad unstable when he grabbed hold of one and pushed his weight down on it. Rust crumbled in his hand and he wiped the orange, russet mess down his trousers.

He turned back to Madison with a look of dismay on his face. "I dunno... they don't seem too sturdy."

Madison looked a little uncertain. "Which one of you two is light--?"

She blanched and looked from Sam, taking in his bulky, muscled six foot three frame to Chloe, with her slim, much smaller figure.

Chloe scoffed, "Ha, please. As if that beast weighs less than I do."

"Yeah. Like your little, weak ass is gonna manage to shift that. You might break a nail. Then what would we do?" Sam placed his hands on his cheeks in mock panic.

"Up yours, dickhead." Chloe half-smiled at him and punched him in the arm.

Madison couldn't help but smile at their witty banter.

"It depends who'd be best. I'd be lighter and better to climb, but Sam would be stronger, better to move the grate," Chloe offered. She sized up the distance between them and the ceiling. "I'd offer to have Sam sit on my shoulders, but I'd be half the size of what I am now after he'd finished."

"You'll have to go on my shoulders, that way you'll have more leverage to move the thing than if you attempted to climb those deathtraps," Sam stated matter-of-factly, nodding at the ladder's treads.

"And what if I can't move the grate?" Chloe countered.

"Well, we won't know how difficult or easy it is until we try it."

Chloe rolled her eyes. "Alright, fine. But no copping a feel."

Sam grinned at her. "The thought never crossed my mind."

"Pfft. Yeah, right."

"Okay, guys, let's do this. We don't have much time." Madison interrupted the pair. "I'm going to manipulate the air in here to stop sound coming through. It means we won't be able to hear each other either, so any problems, Chloe kick Sam on the shoulder, stop what you're doing and I'll bring the sound back. OK?"

Chloe turned to Madison, then to Sam with a wicked smile on her face. Sam groaned, but squatted low so Chloe could climb onto his shoulders. Once perched he slowly stood up.

"Damn, Chlo. There's more to you than meets the eye, ain't there?"

"Pure muscle, baby. Now hurry up and lift me."

"I'm trying, but I feel like my legs are gonna buckle."

"Tut. As if, Sam. Man up, for God's sake."

With a few more moans and groans in protest, Sam lifted Chloe, giving her ample space between head and grate, enough to get a good hold. She signalled Madison for the go-ahead.

They watched the witch close her eyes and raise her arms in Chloe's direction. She began to chant in a whisper before her voice stopped—though her lips still moved. Chloe *felt* the air shift.

Sound disappeared, leaving Madison mute. Opening her eyes, she nodded at Chloe, but Sam tapped her leg regardless.

Chloe pushed on the grate. It shuddered with her efforts, and small flakes of rust and rot fluttered to the ground. Yet no sound escaped—*at least Sam can't hear me struggle,* she thought.

She pushed with everything in her, sweating from the exertion when the grate started to shift, slowly out of place. Sam began to sway underneath her, but she couldn't give up, the grate would fall back into place otherwise.

She persevered through clenched teeth and aching arms. Her stomach tightened against the effort, but the grate kept moving—just a little further and she'd have it free.

*

Sam felt his knees giving way. Not that Chloe weighed a lot—she didn't, despite his earlier comments—but the energy pulled from him under the effort of trying to hold another person's weight for so long. With no indication of Chloe's progress, the whole process seemed even more straining.

Sweat poured from his forehead, dripped down his back—his shirt stuck to him. His legs shook and his neck and back throbbed. His shoulders ached from the brunt of the exercise.

His left leg gave way beneath him and he stumbled forward. Chloe kicked away from him before he took her down, too—in the split second before, the grate must've moved aside, because Chloe hung from the lip of the hole.

Sam watched Chloe struggle at the opening before he twisted his head in Madison's direction. She stared at Sam, still chanting, while he sat on his backside and rubbed his knees.

Returning his gaze to his colleague, he watched Chloe hook an arm over the side of the hole and haul herself up. Before long, she planted her feet on firm ground and peered back into the tunnel. Lifting her head to check her surroundings, she looked back down and gave them both a thumbs up.

A rush of noises hurtled back—water dripped, wind rustled, and, with harsh breathing, Sam grunted, still massaging his knees.

"All clear?" Madison looked up at Chloe.

"Looks like it. I can't see or hear anybody."

Madison nodded, then turned to Sam. "You ready to get up there?"

"How we gonna manage that?" Sam failed to think that far ahead.

Chloe made it safely, but how would they make it up there? He could shoulder lift Madison, but then what about him? Madison tutted at him, shook her head and smiled.

Sam stood on shaky legs when Madison beckoned him. She shut her eyes again and raised her palms toward him. Sam's face screwed up in confusion, before his feet left the ground.

"Holy shit!" he proclaimed.

Sam drifted at a steady pace toward the hole and Chloe moved aside for him. Once near enough, he gripped the edges and lifted himself up, coming to kneel beside his colleague. Barely a breath escaped him before Madison's head emerged through the grate. Within moments, she, too, crouched beside them both.

They were definitely in the dungeon, complete with flaming torches in removable wall sconces and black, metal cages dotted around the large room. The walls were aged brick, yellowed and crumbling in places, vegetation growing in others.

Chloe got up first and pointed out four thick, wooden doors lining the long corridor in front of them, all wide open. Grabbing a torch from the wall beside her, she took careful steps toward the door closest and peered into the room beyond.

She gasped and dropped the torch—the flames spluttered, but didn't die out. She braced herself against the wall, retching before she turned on her heel and expelled the contents of her stomach in the corridor. Sam and Madison made to move, but she put her hand out to stop them while she took deep breaths.

She shook her head in frantic movements, voice trembling. "No… you don't… d-don't go in there."

Sam hesitated, but Madison told him she needed to know what lay beyond the door. She edged past Chloe, who still steadied herself against the rough-bricked wall, spitting out the remains of bile still clinging to her throat.

Madison let out a small scream and fell to her knees. Her hands flew to cover her mouth as tears flowed freely down her ashen face. Sam stepped toward her, her body convulsing with silent sobs.

Neither girl tried to stop him when he sidled past Madison's kneeling form. He forced his attention to whatever disturbed the girls so much, eyes widening, stomach contracting. His body stiffened as he stared at the horror before him.

No windows illuminated the large, bare cell, but Sam clearly saw the three female bodies stacked against the far wall. Every one of them naked, glazed eyes open and staring straight at him—a look of complete terror forever frozen in their dead, vacant stares.

Each woman's throat gaped open, a ragged, bloodied rent. The room stank of the stale blood congealed on the floor in random splashes. But the thing troubling Sam the most were the swollen, pregnant bellies of each victim.

"We have to keep moving." Sam uttered, his dull voice shaking while he struggled to pull his zombie-like gaze away from the carnage before him.

Chloe stood up straight, took a deep breath and wiped her face with the back of her hand. "You're right. We have a job to do, and we'll make sure they pay for this."

Madison attempted to dry her face before Sam managed to haul her to her feet. He tried to comfort her, telling her these witches would pay; that they'd suffer. She stopped crying and straightened. The three of them turned toward the door just about visible at the end of the tunnel.

*

They entered a dimly lit hallway leading off into a large dining room. Dark banks of clouds outside the tall windows cut off any natural light from filtering through. The uncanny silence left behind an uneasy feeling.

Madison tugged at Sam's arm and indicated she would search upstairs. Sam nodded, and both officers watched her body submerge into the inky gloom.

Splitting up seemed a bad idea, but they needed to cover a large area and Madison could take of herself, being able to yell if she ran into trouble or frazzle someone with a bolt of electricity or something.

Once again using the light from their phones, the two officers skirted their way through the dining room. Having seen the blueprints, they knew roughly the way to go; however, the blueprints didn't show the location of furniture. More than once Sam kicked or tripped over something, each time whispering a curse, and each time Chloe delivered a punch to his arm for his clumsiness.

They reached the large set of double doors leading into the living room. Sam stopped to listen, placing his ear to the wood. With a glance at Chloe, he shrugged his shoulders before they both removed their police issue batons—although, what they hoped to achieve with them against a flock of powerful, murderous witches left them clueless. Either way, they opened the doors with silent caution.

Chapter 20

Despite a hurried plan, the Faction's involvement couldn't go further than a thorough sweep of the perimeter and surrounding areas near the mansion, and ensuring none of the witches made a bid to escape unseen.

Unless any of the warriors could manipulate the homeowner's mind, they would need an invitation to enter the premises.

Their only hope remained with Madison and the two officers—that they could flush the witches out of the building and into the gardens where the vampires now waited.

Lucas called over Deacon and Blake to him and alerted them to the only light on in the house, coming from the living room. All other rooms visible from their position were bathed in darkness.

He started to discuss their next move when Blake noticed a light come on in the study. He growled and raced over to the building, Deacon and Lucas followed close behind.

All three ducked underneath the windows to shield themselves from a possible attack, while they could do nothing but stand outside. Blake figured it could be Sam, Chloe or Madison at this point, but none of them were taking any chances.

The door to the study closed behind whoever entered, and Blake risked a quick glance, lifting his head over the large, stone window ledge. His breath caught and his stomach somersaulted into his mouth at the sight of her, caked in darkened blood and limping.

"Amelia!" He banged on the window.

*

The sudden noise startled Amelia. She threw herself behind one of the sofas in the room and braced herself for an attack. Backing against it, her breathing increased, her heart raced while she thought over what to do next. She couldn't head for the door, by the time she managed to heave the massive thing open she could be incinerated. The only other exit led outside, toward the threat.

Before panic could fully set in, she heard her name again, this time registering the voice.

Without further thought, she shot up from behind the sofa and hobbled to the window. Blake's palms pressed against the cold glass and she leaned her head on it, laughing with nerves and relief at the sight of him.

He smiled back at her with joy, hope and longing in his eyes. She turned, and ran to the veranda, pushing the doors open. Throwing caution to the wind, she launched herself into Blake's arms and he littered her face and neck with desperate kisses.

Sliding her down his firm body, he held her back and stared into her eyes.

"Are you hurt? Where are you bleeding from?" His voice came out rushed, panicked. He turned her head this way and that, examined her body for any sign of damage.

"I'm fine, just the usual scrapes and bruises." She offered him a lopsided smile.

"What happened?"

"Darcy's involved. She came for me, I had to... I... ."

She threw herself against him again, trying to hold back tears while Blake wrapped his strong arms around her slim frame. He promised her he would make sure she never came to harm again.

Deacon's voice broke their moment of tranquillity. "Where's Elora?"

Amelia looked up at him and shook her head. "They've taken her somewhere else, but I think I know where." She tried to move, but Blake held her protectively against his chest.

Deacon raced to stand in front of her. "Where?"

One word, but filled with so much panic and fear.

"Cassandra's last name is Hewitt, and--"

"I don't understand what that has to do with anything," Deacon interrupted with exasperation.

Lucas approached with a perplexed expression. "I know that name."

"Inside, I found documents detailing her family history. Her real name isn't even Cassandra, but her last name is definitely Hewitt. I found clippings, portraits, and birth and death records. She's related to Katherine Hewitt."

"Who's Katherine Hewitt?" Blake placed a hand on her shoulder, amid Deacon's increased impatience and unease with every passing moment.

"She was one of the Pendle Hill Witches, burned at the stake in sixteen-twelve. I'll bet anything Cassandra has taken Ellie to Pendle Hill to perform the final sacrifice." Amelia turned her head to the miles of forest covering the Lancashire countryside.

Deacon made a move to tear off, but stilled when a scream sounded and the patio doors to the living room at the opposite end of the house burst open. Chloe, Sam and Madison emerged, racing straight over when they saw Amelia.

Deacon ran past them at lightning speed and disappeared into the thick, surrounding woodlands.

"Shit!" Blake exclaimed. He grabbed hold of Amelia's arms and devoured her mouth with his in a hot, sensuous, knee-trembling kiss, before breaking away to follow Deacon's dust trail.

Amelia blinked a couple of times before Madison, Chloe and Sam approached her.

"Darcy...?" Chloe shifted her gaze between the house and the blood still coating Amelia's shirt, dark against the already crimson material.

Amelia dropped her gaze to the ground and nodded, knowing they would have passed her dead and battered body.

Chloe threw her arms around Amelia's waist and hugged her close. "You did what you had to," she whispered.

Sam attempted a smile, resting a hand on her shoulder.

Chloe released Amelia.

The DCI turned to Lucas as he spoke, "You know where to go, we'll see you there." Then he, too, disappeared amid a blur of rain and gravel.

Everyone looked to Amelia. "I'll explain on the way," she offered, then ran to the waiting vehicles.

∞∞∞

The ear-piercing screech of a nearby owl woke me, but my eyes remained closed, the sound rattled through my fragile head. I tried to force my eyes open, but they refused to take note of anything I commanded them to do. Instead, I tried to squint in an effort to make out my surroundings.

Buffeting winds and beating rain confirmed the outdoors. But it struck me odd; I couldn't feel any of the storm. I expected to feel the wind battering my body, or the rain thrashing against my skin. But nothing.

I pried my eyes open further and spied the flickering of candlelight and blurred shapes ambling about. Someone knelt on the floor not far from me, carving something into the ground.

Vision clearing, I made out Cassandra's thin figure in the middle of a circle of rocks—the same rock formation of my dreams. My heart sank, my bowels nearly following.

Opening my eyes fully, I noted my hands were shackled, the jeans and tee I changed into earlier swapped for a knee-length, white dress. The material clung to my skin, soaked through from the cold, damp earth I lay on. My bare legs felt every bite of the light breeze somehow permeating the protective circle.

Lying still, five voices hummed through my head, whispering. A baby screamed and my mind hurtled back to my nightmare. I sat bolt upright, chained hands shooting instinctively to my belly. Feeling the familiar swell of my baby tucked safe inside, I breathed a sigh of relief. However, the five psychotic witches were now very aware of my current state of consciousness.

"Good evening, Elora. Glad you could join us. You are in for a treat tonight." Cassandra hissed words laced with venom. Her eyes widened and an excited expression flashed across her face in a sadistic manner.

Trying to shake free of my restraints, I raised myself to my knees. "What do you want?"

Laughing again, she bent down close to my face. "Oh, you foolish girl. I thought it would be blatantly obvious by now. I want what you have been holding for me."

Her eyes lit up when she cupped my swollen belly.

I spat in her face. "Get your filthy, fucking hands off my child, you crazy bitch."

She wiped her cheek with the back of her hand, then slapped me around the face with it.

"My, my. Here I was thinking you were some weak, little girl afraid of her own shadow."

I ignored the stinging sensation in my jaw, and turned to face her. Not fancying another slap, I kept my mouth closed and my eyes glaring into the inky depths of hers. She laughed at my silence, the raucous sound jarred my damn nerves. If I could get loose, I'd happily wipe the smug sneer from her face.

I tried to tap into my magic, but I didn't know how to. I understood my emotions often triggered it and I didn't think there could be anything more pure than the fear I felt right now. At the prospect of having my gut sliced open and my baby taken from me and sacrificed, while I lay dying on the ground.

A familiar sensation bubbled inside me, a burn in the pit of my stomach. My fingertips tingled, but every time I tried to force something free it just... fizzled out.

"Darling, you won't get through those cuffs using magic. They're infused with a binding spell." She smiled at me, a knowing curve of her lips.

Invoking the Witch

Vindictive, conniving, self-righteous bitch! I wanted to kill her, throttle her with my own bare hands, but instead I sighed in bitter frustration and hung my head. I felt close to resigning myself to the same fate befalling the witches before me, and the notion made me want to scream until my lungs burst.

Cassandra stalked over to a familiar ditch dead centre of the rock-circle. She drew a knife from beneath her robes and handed it to Keira.

Tears flowed free and fast down my cheeks—hot trails against my cold skin—while Keira knelt. I lurched forward when a cry from the ditch shattered the atmosphere, but my restraints held me back as I struggled against them. Cassandra cackled at my anguish, a hideous, penetrative sound.

My blood began to boil again and my body quaked against my harsh, erratic breathing. My arms went numb and my limbs tingled with pins and needles. The tips of my fingers started to heat. Small sparks fizzed, landing on my skin, but not burning.

All the while that goddamn bitch kept laughing, cajoling me. I wanted her dead. Looking up I saw pure pleasure plastered across her features, an ugly, evil smirk across her face. We both turned our attention back to Keira when she raised the knife above the baby and began her chant.

I screamed a deafening sound—one I didn't think humanly possible. It echoed around the forest startling just about everyone and everything—time stood still, birds scattered, screeching from the safety of their nests, animals scurried away. Cassandra's head snapped in my direction, wide eyed and ruddy, when we heard my chains crumble.

Chapter 21

Deacon hurtled through the woods without stopping to see if his brothers followed. He *needed* to get to Elora the fastest way possible.

The scene around him blurred together, a sombre mix of darkness, trees, bushes and sky all melded into one. Panic and terror drove him faster and faster, all the while he tried to use his senses to hone in on any activity around him.

His skin iced over and he forced down the panic coursing through his blood. She would be OK; he would save her. He would get to her before anyone harmed a hair on her head. *I have to.*

He felt the presence of his kin close by, could hear Sam's bike racing across the countryside. He heard another bike too, slower. Two people on it—someone commandeered Lucas' bike in favour of the cars.

None of this mattered right now, though, because a deafening, almost inhuman scream pierced through the night.

Elora! The beast tore free. *I'll slaughter every fucking one of them?*

His fangs dropped and his vision glazed over with a deep, red mist. He roared a monstrous sound before he crashed through the trees into a clearing. He didn't stop to think before he leapt from the ground and headed straight for the biggest threat—a crouched figure with a knife in her hand.

He smashed into the blonde and the two of them flew across the clearing, straight into a large rock. The knife fell from her hand and managed to slice down the left hand side of her face. Thick rivulets of blood oozed from the cut and the sickly sweet smell overpowered Deacon. It seeped into his senses and clouded his rational mind.

With a feral roar, he sank his teeth into the soft flesh of the witch's neck. She screamed, clawed at him while the warm, ruby fluid gushed down her neck and chest. She passed out, and the moment he realised she no longer posed a threat, Deacon turned away from her. He searched the area for Elora.

She crouched, thirty feet in front of him, on her hands and knees, her back arched while she gulped in lungfuls of air in front of a wide-eyed, scowling Cassandra. The witch didn't seem to even notice him careen through the woods; taking out one of her own while she stood and watched Elora with intent.

Deacon didn't want to afford her the luxury; he jumped up from his stooped position and threw himself at her.

∞ ∞ ∞

Sam realised he wouldn't get any further through the dense woodland, and so discarded his bike. He looked behind for Amelia and Madison—both on Lucas' bike—but saw no immediate sign. Chloe would be even further afield in her car.

A scream tore through the forest and Sam turned and ran toward it.

He didn't make it more than twenty feet, when a strong force knocked him to the ground in a daze. Sam did not expect the blow Daniel dealt him, but he quickly recovered when the robust maniac came back at him for another shot.

Blocking Daniel's next punch with one arm, Sam bought his other smashing into his attacker's face. Blood erupted from Daniel's mouth, but he didn't falter. Instead, he countered with a punch to Sam's stomach. The Detective bent double and Daniel dealt him an elbow to the back of the head.

The blow didn't knock Sam out, but it felled him. He dropped to one knee—one hand resting on the ground. Daniel raised his leg to kick him in the face, but Sam grabbed for it and lifted it high. Daniel fell, winded. Sam lunged for him without a moment's hesitation.

He drove his foot into Daniel's ribs, causing him to double up, roaring in pain. Sam pulled the slighter man up by his collar and smashed his fist into his face, twice before dropping him again.

A shout from Amelia drew his attention. Daniel punched Sam in his knee. The DI cried out with the brute force and crumpled to the floor. Daniel pulled a knife from his belt and knelt over the officer.

"I'm gonna enjoy tearing your guts out, pig," he snarled in Sam's face.

Daniel plunged the blade into Sam's left shoulder. The DI roared in pain and tried to bring his other arm up to punch Daniel in the face. Too slow—Daniel pulled another knife and thrust it into the right shoulder.

A second howl tore through Sam, and a third knife aimed for his heart.

"*A bestia!*"

A commanding voice erupted somewhere to Sam's left and a strong gust of wind tousled his hair and clothes before blasting Daniel away from him. The property developer thudded to the ground and skidded heavily into a tree, head first. Amelia's face came into view, hovering over Sam's skewered body.

"I have to get these out. They've got you pinned."

"No shit, Sherlock," Sam grunted through gritted teeth. "Do what you have to."

He squeezed his eyes shut before Amelia pulled the daggers from his body. He let out an agonised cry, each knife sliding with infinite torture out of the wound. Through his haziness, he watched Madison bend over him and apply pressure to the injuries.

"Don't move," she soothed. "They're not life-threatening, but you're gonna feel the sting for a while."

She offered a half-apologetic, half-weary smile at her attempt at humour.

"Stay with him." Amelia patted Madison's back, but before Sam could protest, she shot up and ran further into the forest.

∞ ∞ ∞

Deacon took Cassandra to the ground with a nauseating thud and plunged his fangs into the supple skin of her shoulder. She cried out, flailing her arms, clawing at his shirt. Elora screamed beside him and shouted his name.

Jerking his head to the side, he saw her. Her beautiful, pale face moist. Her rose-blushed lips quivered while her chestnut eyes sparkled with crystalline tears.

A bright, white bolt struck him in the chest and sent him hurtling backward. He crashed to the ground, winded.

"Heathen scum!"

Deacon twisted his head to see Laila pull a vial of murky liquid from between her ample cleavage. She threw the concoction at Deacon's feet where it smashed on impact. Ink black tendrils raced up and encircled him, trapping him while he struggled against them.

Grasping at her oozing wound, Cassandra walked over. "Now you get to watch as I kill your little bitch." She spat the words at him before turning around to face a stricken Elora.

Cassandra stalked over to her and kicked her in the face. Elora grunted and tumbled to the side, arms outstretched to brace her fall. Deacon rumbled a guttural, monstrous sound.

Cassandra advanced again.

Elora threw her hand out, a bolt of charged electricity shooting from her fingertips, narrowly missing Cassandra's head. A few loose strands of the witch's ebony hair fizzled and smouldered, but it did not stop her.

"Someone's coming into their powers." Cassandra knelt beside Elora and addressed her confused glare. "You don't even know who you are, do you?"

"Your worst fucking nightmare," she screamed, head-butting the witch and hauling herself up to deliver a right hook to her face.

A roaring growl erupted behind her, stealing her attention. Blake and Lucas crashed through the clearing and Cassandra seized her moment. She lunged at Elora's throat, and took them both hurtling into a tree; her grip tightening.

∞∞∞

Lucas headed for Serena. The wig-wearing witch closed her eyes and spat out foreign words.

"Mortis infligit in inmortuis!"

An orange ball shot from her fingertips and expanded on its course for Lucas. The agile vampire dived out of the way, feeling the heat sear the exposed flesh of his arms. The amber sphere hit a tree and exploded into bright, red flames, licking up the bark, sparks jumping from one branch to another. A loud roar rumbled through his chest and escaped his mouth. His fangs dropped.

Serena's face paled when Lucas landed in front of her. Grabbing her shaking shoulders, he spun her around. She thrust her hands toward his head, clawing desperately, but before she could utter another spell, the vampire plunged his fangs into and across her bare neck. Blood ebbed in ruby rivers from the shredded wounds.

Lucas tore out her throat before he threw her to the ground, gulping down the sweet reward of his kill, licking his lips.

He rounded on his next target, but Laila flung herself on his back and stabbed him in the shoulders and neck with a sharp instrument. Lucas roared and grappled with the small woman, trying to reach out and throw her from him. Pain exploded from him with every penetration and blood drenched his grey T-shirt. His vision blurred.

*

Blake bolted for the raven-haired Priestess, but someone careened into him, grabbed him by the neck and took him to the ground.

"Now it's time to finish what I started." The hate-filled eyes of Ember stared back at him.

Only this Ember's strength bellied her age and abilities. At two hundred and eighty years old, Blake should've easily overpowered a one hundred and three year old Ember without any effort at all. But he struggled to free himself from her tight grip.

"Stake him," a voice shouted from behind.

Ember thrust her hand out and caught the long, wooden missile thrown at her with her free hand. She didn't take her glaring eyes off Blake's.

A lunatic smile grew on her face when she bought the stake plummeting down.

∞∞∞

Amelia burst into the fray amid broken branches and flying leaves. Seeing a maniacal vampire holding a stake above *her* man, she mustered all her speed and strength before she flung herself into Ember and rugby-tackled her to the ground.

Amelia gained the upper hand and straddled Ember's torso and arms.

"Get off me, you bitch," the young vamp squealed, writhing in the dirt.

Amelia's chuckle died in her throat when Ember bought her legs up, wrapped them around the DCI's head and launched her into the air. Amelia landed with a thud in front of Ember, who wasted no time in advancing on her.

Winded, and trying to scramble away, Amelia grunted when the unnaturally strong creature delivered a powerful kick to her ribs, which sent her reeling on to her back. She cried out at the fresh agony lancing through her.

With pain-clouded vision, Amelia watched Blake charge toward them, but Ember threw her hand out and screamed something incoherent. Blake's body lurched before being thrown back into the distance with a shot of red energy bursting from Ember's palm. Amelia stared, wide-eyed, at the scene before her—*no fucking way. Did a vampire just use magic?*

Chapter 22

I closed my eyes and fought off death, barely registering my surroundings.

Cassandra's strong grip defied her frail image, and my lungs screamed at me to breath. While an assortment of emotions streamed through me, I couldn't latch on to any one of them, in order to zap this crazy bitch off me.

"I have been waiting for this day for a long time, "Cassandra sneered, her teeth bared. "Once you're dead, my granddaughter's sacrifice will finally give me everything I want."

She ran a heavy hand over my stomach and I blanched. *Her* granddaughter? My struggles diminished and I heaved.

"That's right, my precious." Her lip twitched and her nostrils flared. "I have no idea what my son first saw in you, but I'm glad he came around to my line of thinking."

I couldn't breathe. And not because Cassandra's grasp tightened around my throat, but because it all started to make perfect sense. *Daniel is Cassandra's son.* I couldn't believe my ears. All this time... his behaviour, the violence. My pregnancy. It had all been part of some sick, twisted plot, cooked up between demented mother and son.

But why?

Sight and sound intermingled into one distorted haze, but I would not be beaten. My baby depended on me and I wouldn't let her down. She needed me, now more than ever and I would *not* let this... fucking bitch get her hands on *my* child.

She could go straight back to the murky depths of the hell she'd emerged from.

A wave of energy stirred deep within, itching to break free. The intensity grew, bubbling like a scorching volcano on the verge of erupting. My eyes snapped open and my body bucked and vibrated. A searing white light burst from me, bathing my whole being. The force knocked Cassandra back and she smashed straight into Ember.

I crashed to my knees and sucked in deep, beautiful, coveted breaths of air. Amelia scrambled up and ran over to me, crouching before she asked how I felt.

I swallowed past the burn in my throat, "I'm good, help the others." I waved her off, assuring her I'd be fine.

She stole a quick glimpse in Deacon's direction and, realising she couldn't do anything, headed for Lucas as he battled with a lunatic witch stabbing at his shoulders.

Glancing back, I caught Deacon's stare, desperation in his imploring eyes. I closed mine—needing to do *something*— and I tried to block out everything around me, focused on drawing my powers. Tears fell fast and heavy down my cheeks before my body shot up to my knees, hands outstretched either side of me, back arched.

Shock persisted when a burning—neither painful nor uncomfortable—enveloped my eyes, bright light emanated from my whole being. I couldn't see myself, but I *knew* the white light bathed me in its brilliance. I *sensed* it.

My body didn't belong to me in this moment; something took control, flinging my arms forward. Light surged from my splayed fingertips and rushed straight for Deacon with immeasurable speeds. It circled the black fog in a cacophony of demonic, defeated screeching. I slammed my hands over my ears, but couldn't tear my gaze from the struggling, squirming mist before the light completely devoured it.

Deacon rushed before me. On one knee, he took my face in his hands, looked into my eyes, concern across his features. "Have they hurt you?"

It took a second or two for sound to filter back to me. I clutched my belly, but I shook my head, trembling while he wrapped me in a tight embrace.

∞ ∞ ∞

Amelia grabbed hold of Laila's short, dark hair and yanked her away from Lucas. Both girls fell to the ground in a tangle of flailing arms and legs, ignoring an almighty *whoosh* erupting from nearby.

Extricating themselves from one another, Amelia righted herself quicker. She slammed a left fist into the witch's stomach, then swung a powerful right hook into her jaw. Laila dropped. Amelia landed on her and punched her face over and over.

Lindsey Jayne

A bright light, with all the force of a burning fireball, distracted the DCI for a brief moment. Laila used the opportunity to launch her fist up and connected with Amelia's jaw with a sickening crack, knocking her to the ground. Laila flew at her and smacked her again while she lay, dazed, on her back.

The white light vanished, but it still burned Amelia's retinas. She struggled to gain recognition of Laila above her as she held a knife against her throat.

The blade sliced a nick in the DCI's flesh before the witch sailed off her. Clambering to her elbows, Amelia watched Chloe body slam a prone Laila. All too late, Amelia saw the glint of the dagger's blade before Laila thrust it up. Chloe slammed into it with force enough to snap it off at the hilt.

"NO!" Amelia scrambled to her feet.

Chloe lay—unmoving—over Laila, blood trickled from her mouth and her eyes rolled back. Laila forced her off and the Sergeant thudded to the ground.

Amelia rushed over, fuelled by anger and hatred, and lifted her foot, slamming it into Laila's face before she could get up. The witch crashed back down, head cracking off the firm ground before Amelia drew back and stomped on her face, again and again until strong arms pulled her away.

She stared down at Laila's battered remains. Her nose a smashed-up, bloody pulp, teeth scattered across the dirt, eyes swollen shut and a deep rent in the side of head exposed bone and brain matter.

Shaking loose of Blake's hold, Amelia stepped over the witch's motionless form and dropped to her knees beside her friend. Chloe coughed and spluttered, blood pooled down her chin. Amelia grabbed her and cradled her in her lap, stroking her hair.

Chloe coughed again. "You got the bitch, right?"

Amelia choked on a short laugh—a hollow, sad sound. "Yeah, Chlo. I got the bitch." She stopped stroking her hair and looked deep into Chloe's glazed eyes. "You saved my life."

Chloe smiled. "And I'd do it again, too."

The Sergeant's eyes rolled back, her body went limp and her head fell to the side.

Amelia clutched Chloe to her chest and cried out.

Lucas sought out Ember the moment Amelia pulled the flailing witch off of him. He spied her, crouched behind a large rock. She caught his eye and snarled—fangs down—daring him to take his best shot with a 'come hither' motion of her hand.

Focusing on her superior, Ember muttered something indiscernible and cast a hand out in front of her. A wall of flame erupted from the ground behind Lucas, blocking them off from the rest of the fray. Lucas threw her a stunned glance when he heard the *whoosh* of the flames and Ember used the opportunity to attack. She drew a silver blade from her black boot and flung herself at him.

Lucas turned too late; Ember knocked him off his feet and stabbed her knife into his chest with a scream. She missed his heart by mere inches. Lucas roared out in pain and laid open her face with his hand before he threw her off him with renewed vigour. She landed with a heavy clump against one of the large rocks and grunted when the wind escaped her lungs.

The warrior leapt off his feet and sailed through the air. He drew a sword from a concealed sheath and descended upon her. Horror marred her otherwise pretty features and Lucas smiled viciously at her, lips curling up to bare his fangs while she scrambled further up the rock.

Lucas landed and thrust his sword, aiming for her heart. Ember shifted, throwing herself to the side before she chucked a glass bottle to the ground. Smoke engulfed her and she vanished amid a plume of hazy grey—the wall of fire died out, the very moment another pained scream echoed through the night.

Chapter 23

I surveyed the devastation surrounding me, tears streaming down my face.

Is it over?

The sounds of battle and death ceased, but I still felt on edge. A million questions tumbled through my mind.

I stood up slowly, Deacon aiding me, and walked into the middle of the circle. After everything kicked off, I forgot a baby lay among us.

I stared at him, wriggling around in the shallow ditch—oblivious, and unharmed by the devastation.

Reaching down, I scooped him out and caught sight of Amelia. She lifted her head to look at me.

She lowered an unmoving Chloe to the ground with such gentle care—reluctant to leave her—and stood up. Blake moved to help her, but she refused his assistance and paced over to Lucas, head held high with each purposeful stride. My heart ached for them and their obvious loss.

Amelia stepped over the prone body of Serena and stood beside the tall warrior.

He faced her, the sad look in his gaze betraying his rigid stance. Amelia held her hand out and Lucas gave her his sword.

"You sure?" he asked her.

Amelia nodded.

She stalked over to Laila and, in one fluid movement, swung the sword down and took off Laila's head—just like that.

She ambled back to Lucas and handed him his blade before she returned to Chloe's lifeless form.

Lucas strode over to Serena's inert body and lopped her head off.

A rustling in the trees to my right drew my attention, then movement to my left. I looked over—briefly registering no sign of Ember or Cassandra—before a blonde blur flew at me.

Kiera drew a dagger and raised it above her head, her bloodied face contorted into a mask of fury;

lips peeled back baring red-stained teeth. She looked like a savage, salivating beast.

I clutched the child to my chest and braced myself, but before she reached me a furry shape shot past my face—course hair bristled against my flesh and I rocked back and forth on my feet, maintaining my balance. It charged into Keira with a nauseating thud and both woman and beast crashed to the ground.

A large, brown wolf took an angry swipe at Keira's face, growling over her cries of pain. Blood sprayed the rock and ground beside them in fast, thick splatters. He roared in her face—his eyes sparking a fiery orange— before he bared his jowls and ripped her throat out.

Another furred animal shot past the first, and the silver-grey bulk of another wolf ran howling into the trees, while the brown one stalked away from his kill. Amid pops and crunches, the wolf's body twisted, his hair retracted and he transformed into a muscled, butt-naked man right before my eyes.

Nate!

"Better late than never." He winked, blood smeared across his scruffy face.

He sauntered toward us and snagged a discarded piece of white cloth from the ground. He wrapped it around his waist.

Lucas walked steadily over to Keira while she gasped and floundered on the ground, like a fish out of water. He barely looked at her when he swiped his sword across her neck.

∞ ∞ ∞

Back at the Compound, Amelia listened, while Nate informed everyone that Daniel managed to escape. While Madison had tended to Sam's wounds, he disappeared. Ember scarpered, too, along with Cassandra. They left little trace of themselves behind, but Amelia would find them—she vowed to. A sentiment shared by all.

She went to see Sam—holed up in the hospital wing with his injuries; arms in thick bandages, his face a mass off black and purple bruising.

He took the news of Chloe's death hard.

"I keep replaying the images over and over in mind," Amelia sobbed, "like some homemade, low-budget slasher move. I can't force them out."

Her guard resolved, and she cried, leaning into Sam's bare chest as he pulled her close, shedding his own audible sobs, unashamed and completely devastated.

Unable to stop herself, she'd left Sam on the ward to go see Chloe in the morgue. Her remains were to be cremated, her ashes given to her parents.

Amelia stood, beside herself with grief, but broke down again when Sebastian removed the cover from Chloe's untarnished face—he did a good job patching her up. Despite the pallid complexion and pale blue lips, she looked peaceful, but it did nothing for Amelia's feelings of utter desolation at the loss of her co-worker. Her friend.

Tears streamed freely down her face, and she took the white cover from Sebastian and drew it back across Chloe's eternally resting body.

*

I wanted to ask a thousand and one questions when we returned to the Compound, but my mind went blank. We walked into the living area where my dad sat, waiting, by the fire. He nursed a glass of amber liquid between his palms.

When he saw us enter, he dropped the tumbler and ran at me, wrapping me in a tight embrace.

I fell into him, weak and confused.

Deacon's welcome hand spread across my lower back and eased me toward the sofas. I grabbed my dad's hand and pulled him along with me.

All but Lucas and Deacon left my dad and me to talk.

Words didn't come easy. I didn't know where to begin.

After Dad told me he didn't know my mother was a witch, but loved her all the same, I asked the General the only thing my brain would allow me to digest.

"Why did you cut off their heads?"

He looked between me and Deacon, probably unsure of whether or not he heard me right. I wasn't ready for anything more, yet, so I widened my eyes and nodded once at him to answer.

"Um… well, witches can die from severe injuries, but they do so at a slower rate than regular humans. They have a higher threshold for pain and endurance. But even though they die, the level of power they possess means they can reincarnate."

"No shit," I breathed.

"They don't always come back human, and they don't always have their memories intact. But they'll return with the same alignment; if they're evil, they come back as something evil. Often, something much worse than before.

"The body they inhabit is a vessel, and in order to stop them coming back, they must be beheaded and the vessel burned."

It explained why the Faction burned the bodies on the Hill before we left.

I took a deep breath. "What did you find out about my mother?"

Nausea heated my chest and my body trembled.

Deacon held me close, while Lucas explained my heritage to us.

He told us that my mother was a Superior Priestess. She held a power like none other; she could manipulate all the elements and communicate with nature. When she died, I became Superior Priestess; in theory. But because my mother wasn't around to teach me, and my dad had no clue, my powers went untapped.

I would, now, need to be taught how to use my gifts. I didn't know whether to feel excited or downright petrified. My daughter would inherit magic, and it would be up to me to teach her how to use it.

A large part of me felt elated. I shared a special bond with a mother I never knew, and I would get to share that same connection with my child. But it still didn't answer why Cassandra went to such great lengths to make sure I was involved in her elaborate, murderous scheme.

"Why do you have a newspaper article on Isobel?"

Everyone turned their attention to my dad. He held the clipping of Daniel's dad's death between his fingers.

"You know her?" Lucas moved closer to him.

My father's face paled as he stared at the article, before glaring at Lucas. "She cared for my wife during her final days."

I looked at the picture of Isobel Compton and gasped.

"Elora?" Dad placed a hand on my knee.

I covered my mouth with my hand and murmured, "That's Cassandra."

*

I sat in a brilliant-white room, on a white couch covered in red, satin cushions.

I wore a crimson, knee-length gown made from the most exquisite silk. The material caressed my body with such a sensuous trace. The air around me smelled of tulips and violets, and I closed my eyes against the calm solitude.

"Elora."

My eyes snapped open as the voice hummed through my subconscious.

"Yes, mother?" I stared at the white wall in front of me, my lips unmoving.

She floated through the wall. Her ruby red lips, smiling, stark against the smoothness of her ivory skin. Chocolate tresses danced in waves around her shoulders, and bright, blue eyes sparkled with unshed tears.

Against her breast, and wrapped in pure, white silk, she carried her granddaughter.

"I miss you, sweet angel," she whispered, softly.

A single tear escaped the corner of my eye and trailed a warm path down my cheek. "I miss you, too."

She looked down at her granddaughter and smiled. Two crystal tears fell from her eyes and landed on two, tiny hands as they reached for her face.

My mother closed her eyes and whispered, "I'll be with you always."

A glittering cloud shrouded her body and my mother disappeared behind a bright, white light. I shielded my eyes against the brilliance. Turning back, a small, silver speck flickered before me. It darted around my head and shoulders before disappearing behind the read material of my dress.

I embraced my swollen belly as a welcoming warmth enveloped every inch of me.

I closed my eyes and smiled.

My eyes flickered open, struggling against the bright sun bathing my room in a delicious, golden glow. I lay still for a moment, my hands around the swell of my stomach.

Last night, I had teetered on the precipice of death and come out on top. No longer a weak, submissive shadow, I possessed the strength to end this chapter of my life.

A new chapter opened. And with it, a whole new set of mysteries remained unsolved.

But one thing I knew for certain, a part of my mother would always be with me. She gave me the strength to find out the truth. And I would.

Cassandra and Daniel were still out there. They would still come for me. Cassandra knew my mother… once upon a time. Perhaps they'd even been friends. But something in their pasts led Cassandra down a destructive path, a path that involved me and my child, and I wouldn't stop digging that past up until we were both safe.

∞∞∞

Walking out of her office, Amelia flicked the lights off. She didn't sleep one wink after last night's events, and only came to the station to submit her account of what happened. She'd struggled to hold it together when she'd outlined the events of Chloe's death and everything before and after.

She called Chloe's parents and broke the news—cried with them, sensed their world come crashing down around them.

Closing her door, she felt a presence beside her.

"Ellis, a word." DCS Riley Thomas' usual booming voice took on a softer tone.

Will this day ever end? After a gruelling afternoon, Amelia wanted to visit Sam then climb into bed—she missed being able to sleep a whole night without interruption. Though she doubted she'd be able to sleep again for some time.

Sighing, she turned back around and flicked the light switch on again, bathing her office in a yellow/orange luminance.

"Yes, sir?"

"I'm sorry for your loss. For *our* loss. Roberts was a fantastic officer."

"Thank you, sir." Amelia looked at him and her eyes welled up.

"If there's anything I can do… " He stared back at her with equal sadness in his hooded gaze.

"I appreciate that, sir, but I'll be fine."

Attempting a smile, Amelia caught the golden glint in Thomas' eye before he walked away.

∞∞∞

An early dusk settled outside, but I needed some fresh air. Deacon told me Amelia would be here soon to see Sam. I wanted to thank her for her part in saving my life last night, and everything in between.

I liked Amelia, I respected her feisty, gutsy attitude and everything she stood for. People like her made me feel safe. I hoped we'd become friends.

I made my way down to the foyer, forcing a smile at Wendy. She'd resumed her post behind her bank of computers, after having hidden from sight during the ambush earlier last night. She offered her own smile, knowing compassion set behind her tired eyes.

"Has Amelia arrived yet?" I asked her.

"Not yet, hun. She should be here any minute, though."

Wendy buzzed me out the main door.

Stepping into the sticky, humid night, I actually felt refreshed at being able to feel it for what it was. A breeze whistled past me and I closed my eyes, sucking in a deep lungful. I could smell everything—the trees, the flowers, the air itself, and something I couldn't quite pinpoint, something spicy and musky. I forgot about it when I heard Amelia call out to me.

"Ellie!" Her voice cracked, but she threw me a half-smile behind a quick wave.

I exhaled a heavy breath at her tear-stained face, her eyes red and swollen—my heart went out to her.

The first sets of gates opened and I stilled in front of her. She moved to swipe her ID card along the mechanism on the second gate, but stopped and stared at my face.

A cold blast hit me and energy built up inside me, preparing itself for the unknown. I dropped my arms to my sides and stared past Amelia.

"Ellie...?" The DCI's face paled.

A figure emerged from the shadows with lightning speed.

"Daniel?!" A sickness swirled in my stomach.

He grabbed a stunned Amelia before she registered his presence. Drawing a knife from his belt, he positioned it over the side of her throat while he clutched her in a vice-like grip.

"I want that baby, Elora. I'll kill everyone you know and love until you give it up to me," he snarled.

Jesus fucking Christ, he's got fangs!

I shook my head in utter disbelief. This couldn't be happening. "Daniel, y-you're--"

"I mean it Ellie. And so you know just how much, I'll demonstrate my point right now."

He plunged the knife into Amelia's neck.

I screamed. I screamed so hard my throat tore. I sank to my knees and watched Daniel pull the deadly weapon out before he disappeared into the night once more.

Amelia dropped to the floor. Blood pulsed from her neck in thick spurts while she uselessly tried to stem the flow. I hurled myself at the gates and clung to the bars. Her eyes rolled to the back of her head as a growing crimson puddle pooled beneath her. I screamed again and again until I thought I'd be sick, and still I carried on.

"Open the goddamn gates," I cried at the top of my lungs and banged my palms against the steel bars. *Where the fuck are the guards?*

A shape rushed past me and leapt over the gates with no effort at all. Blake hovered over Amelia's dying form. Grabbing hold of her, he clutched her to his chest and roared a barbaric, primal sound.

Collapsing to the floor, I felt Deacon's arms wrap around my waist.

Then, my water broke.

To be continued...

In book 2

Conquering the Witch

About the author

Lindsey lives in England in a little place known as Wolverhampton with her darling Bedlington Terrier, Huxley.

Whilst she does love to read and write, she is still financially challenged because she likes to buy expensive things that she likely doesn't need, with money that she definitely doesn't have! And so, to make ends meet she is employed as a Recruitment Consultant.

But when she is not indulging in a spot of retail therapy, she can usually be found glued to some form of computer, playing one 'shoot 'em up' game or another! She also likes painting, photography and shopping... oh yes, that was mentioned already, right?!

She's not a complete hermit though, she also loves to spend time with her family and friends doing any number of socially acceptable (most of the time) things.

She is a huge fan of paranormal. Thrillers and erotic fiction. And if all three are combined, she is in heaven. Especially when it comes to Alpha males!!!

Keep up to date with new releases and giveaways by visiting:

http://www.facebook.com/LindseyJayneWriter

or follow her on Twitter:

http://twitter.com/LindseyJ_Author

Printed in Great Britain
by Amazon